DICK SNYDER

BINGO

A JONAS
KIRK MYSTERY

authorHOUSE®

AuthorHouse™
1663 Liberty Drive
Bloomington, IN 47403
www.authorhouse.com
Phone: 1 (800) 839-8640

Cover by Jimmy Gibbs

Published by AuthorHouse 01/09/2019

ISBN: 978-1-5462-6524-5 (sc)
ISBN: 978-1-5462-6522-1 (hc)
ISBN: 978-1-5462-6523-8 (e)

Library of Congress Control Number: 2018912614

Print information available on the last page.

This book is printed on acid-free paper.

CONTENTS

REMARKS

My thanks to Susan Reed for introducing me to lottery bingo, from which this story emerged.

My thanks to Maurine Ratekin for her early and steady encouragement of my writing.

My thanks to Paul Magee with whom I share a confident, critical, and collegial eye for one another's work.

My love and deep appreciation for my wife, Linda, who accepts my mental diversions with mild amusement, holding in abeyance negative comment or critical body language.

Dick Snyder
2018

INTRODUCTION

Having solved a series of murders in Woodland Park, Kirk begins to question his pledge to balance the scales of justice. He takes himself to a frozen settlement in Alaska, bonds with a local Indian tribe and learns how it disciplines individual misbehavior. Impressed, he integrates those values into his mantra for punishing homicide, describing himself as nature's alter ego.

He returns to Woodland Park to find himself missed...and needed. New people, new religions, new activities all lead to a series of gambits by interested parties. Sikhs want to build a gurdwara. Catholics want Bingo to balance their budget. Devlin grouses at inadequate police staffing. Bishop Leland Burkey desperately maneuvers to bolster church attendance...and his reputation.

Even as winners file out of the Bingo hall happy and laughing, dark nights witness unsolved robberies. Conversations become uneasy. Business leadership wants safety, growth and profit. Devlin struggles to reassure the community.

Of all the worries, nothing triggers such intense gossip as the death of a nameless, homeless man in a dark alley behind *Stone Cold Charity*. Devlin keeps key evidence secret. Kirk sorts through his options.

FIRST NIGHTER

N-33

Black...not a color but a mood, maybe a tone, sometimes a drape over a difficult moon. In a deep tunnel, a wink of light. A knife moves in a silent quick thrust. He felt the edge, screamed, grasped for his assailant, ripped cloth and staggered. Turning toward the streetlights, he took four halting steps, slumped to the ground. A snippet of life severed and set aside.

The quiet man hid the knife in his clothes, bent over, placed a note inside the clump of rumpled clothing. It read: Allah Akbar!

Geraldine Wright paused. She thought she heard a cry somewhere in the distance...shrill...maybe a rabbit meal for the night owl. She stood still, cocked her head as though aligning a wall hanging. Paused. Nothing. A part of the natural world. The transition from dusk to night continued in silence. Reassured, she stepped up and opened the doors of the parish hall.

Both shy and soaring sounds filled the brightly lit space, and she filed the scene under the tab of "just right". She expected the first Bingo Night at St. Marks's Hall to be well attended. Why not? Edge of winter, middle of the

1

week. Not everyone wanted to be out on the ice sipping brandy or hanging around bicyclists planning their annual spring ride to Duluth. No wind in here. No smoke either. Nice to get out of the house, jingle some coin, maybe put some folding money in her pocket.

She moved about the tables, gliding, looking for a safe seat where she could gather gossip, scan people and spread a story or two. Considering her reputation as a Woodland Park busybody, it took her awhile, but she found space next to Sharon Cunningham. For years a friend, now a confidant, Sharon kept Geraldine's curiosity fueled with rumor and insight.

She spoke as she sat. "Sharon, I can't believe that Father Eggert actually let himself get roped into a hustle like this? What the hell are Catholics doing...gambling for charity. Sounds a little dicey to me... snake eyes maybe, eh?" she smiled.

Sharon looked up, "Hi Deeni. Good to see you coming in out of the cold and dark...Father Eggert? I think he may have more on his plate than just charity. He's been at this parish a while now...he's beginning to get a little edgy. Church attendance seems to be erratic and you know what that means for the weekly collection."

"Restlessness...money shortfalls...well I can see that, but tell me, where the hell is he gonna go... what options does he have?"

"Not sure, Deeni, but a lot of people in St. Mark's wonder why he's not a monsignor. Been a vacancy there in our diocese for quite a while. Puts a lot of pressure on the parish. Bishop Burkey is great at posturing, but not much of an administrator."

"Incompetent I would say...like a lot of people in leadership these days, Sharon. Hell, even the City Council can't seem to get off the pot and solve its income problems...just sits there and talks...tiresome."

"Can't argue with that. I think the parish is going to have to save itself. At the last Altar Society meeting, I caught a few words from Father Eggert's conversation on the phone to Bishop Burkey. Something about 'we will, one way or the other...Bingo will fund it'."

"Oh, yeah? Fund what? A Bingo collection for the poor ending up in a separate basket? Happens all the time."

Sharon looked thoughtful, "Well, you may be right. After dealing with the Church in India, I'm a lot more cautious about buying anything Bishop Burkey is promoting."

"That had to be terrible, Sharon...loving and working with Father Lockhart, building a mission in a Hindu community and then having him die on you while you were on a rest break back home. Never did understand what killed him... they just said sudden death, overnight. Heart attack I guess...you ever hear anything more?"

Sharon paused, chose her words carefully. "You know, Deeni...the way the Church handled all of that left me a little empty. Burkey certainly didn't welcome me when I came home for vacation. Cut me out of the information loop completely and then when news arrived, he treated me like I was Mary Magdalene. Tough time...for weeks. All I ever heard was that Father Lockhart went to bed, went to sleep and didn't wake up. I miss him...really miss him...always will I guess."

"Love and loss, Sharon. I told you at the time. Don't second guess yourself. Hell, you found what you wanted... just didn't end the way you hoped."

"Easy to say, Deeni, but I've heard you. I'm moving on."

"Well good. Now whaddya think of the crowd here...plenty of faces, and I'll bet there's a lot of folding money ready to be a part of the game. Just think...Bingo...who would have thought it would draw a crowd like this. Laughs, luck, and loose cash goin' to a good cause. Fun evening. Maybe Father Eggert found a good strategy...say, who's that guy up there near the basket...I don't recognize him, and I thought I knew everybody in town...is he gonna be the emcee?"

Sharon looked up toward the stage, "Oh, that's Tracy Metzger. Brought in from Cedar Rapids, Iowa to be the face of the fund-raiser. Salesman type I suppose, but he seems genuine enough. We had a good look at his credentials at the last Altar Society meeting. Nothing but good news on him."

"No one is really only good news, Sharon. Must be some kind of gossip about him, eh?"

"Alice Goodwin...she's the new Altar Society president you know...well, she said she heard Burkey talking about Metzger to someone on the phone. Found it very reassuring.

"So, what did she hear?"

"Oh, something like, *'Ah, Metzger, yes...yes...never a scare. I heard about Devlin. Perfect. Will give Tracy the word. Hard worker...always in the soup...wish there were more like him...a good fella, (laughter), not like a fly...it's certainly in his interest. He'll do it, I'm sure. We'll just take the dice."*

"What the hell does all that mean?" Deeni asked, *'heard about Devlin...in the soup...a fly...we'll take the dice?'* Is he accusing my man of gambling?"

"Oh, no Deeni. You know Alice doesn't hear well. He may have said, 'always in the loop' or 'we'll just be nice'. But she seemed to be convinced that the Bishop really liked him."

"Based on what? We know that Alice Goodwin is one of God's great works of humanity, but what does she actually hear? I once said to her, 'What on earth', only to have her ask me *what I liked about Perth*."

"Well...speak directly to her face...she does well when you do that."

"Maybe...well, what do you know about ol' Metzger here?"

"From what I hear, some thru Alice and some from Father Eggert, he worked in Sioux City early on, then moved to Des Moines, finally to Cedar Rapids. Seemed to be a big hit with everyone down there...and lots of comments about his dedication to the Church. Bishop Burkey was really quite taken with him."

"Sounds good, but then one really doesn't know, eh? Married?

"No, but still... nice to have a new man in town."

"Well, I'll have Chester take a good look at him...I'm always curious about strangers."

"Putting the cops on a new face doesn't sound so friendly, Deeni."

"Oh, some police have a winsome way about them," she smiled.

Sharon laughed lightly, "So how're you and Lieutenant Devlin doing these days anyway? Still finding time to slip out of town?"

"Hell yes. I'm not sure who is really keeping track of us, but I don't much care. Chester is a bit more cautious...doesn't want me to be associated with any case investigations, but he sure does like our getaways. Never thought that Winona could provide a hideout for such fun. Damn, he is something...I like him."

"Is he coming over this evening?"

"He said he would. You know the department has a lot of stress to deal with...shortfall in budget, no new hires. They've begun to cut back on night staff on the streets. Some nights, there's no patrol at all after midnight."

"Well, I hope he makes it. Way he moves his bulk about speaks authority...keeps everyone relaxed and comfortable. Hard to think of anything going wrong with him around...hey, I see him now! Gonna make room for him?"

"Oh, hell no! Last thing he wants is us being seen together. I'll bet he scarcely looks this way, and that's fine with me. I'm gonna buy two more cards and get all six of them set up. Ol' Chester boy can find his own place...I'll compare notes with him tomorrow."

"Well, it would be nice if Mr. Bingo got out here and started calling out balls...s'posed to start at 7 and here it is, nearly 7:15...I want to have some fun...oh here he is!"

Up on the stage, Father Eggert apologized to Tracy Metzger for the Bishop's late arrival, told him to just make the introduction, and then he, Eggert, would take it from there.

"No problem," Metzger said, "Schedules are made for breaking." He faced the crowd, called for attention and asked Bishop Leland Burkey to offer a special blessing for the Bingo project.

The Bishop, waiting behind the stage curtain, arranged his sash and shook out his gown, allowed the crowd to look for him...waited a full eight seconds. Murmurs. Then, he slipped into view, glittering in new vestments, heightened with a colorful miter, carrying his crozier, the staff of authority. He pounded the tall, decorative pole firmly on the stage twice to gather silence. Satisfied, he struck the floor with it again, more lightly this time, and handed it to an altar boy.

He perused the crowd, satisfied. Rolled his eyes to heaven and thanked the Lord for providing so many souls to support this important event. He rolled a few r's and fixed his sight on a stranger. "Herrrre, God rrrreceives the gifts of his flock, focuses on theirrrrr holiness and offerrrrs in rrrrreturn his gift of love. Enjoy the night. Support charity. Go in peace."

That should do it, he thought.

He didn't linger. He took the staff and struck it twice more, nodded slightly in the general direction of important people he may have seen and quietly slipped back behind the curtains.

Tracy saw him off the stage and then called on Father Eggert.

Eggert spoke in his warmest voice, "Let me welcome all of you, including our Lutheran soulmates, to St. Mark's Bingo. In the spirit offered by our new Pope Francis, let me also extend a greeting to some of our Muslim and Sikh friends who are here to share fellowship...though not to gamble." He smiled, paused, continued.

"Money is a necessary resource for us to do God's work," he continued, "Sometimes it takes a little extra effort to help us make ends meet. As many of you know, homelessness has begun to grow in Woodland Park, and we are running out of food bank resources. Winter forces us to find shelter for those in need and we need to house several dozen people in the next few weeks. So, simply put, we need more money to 'love our neighbor'. A game of chance should give us the resources we need to soften the edges of the streets...and I must confess...to ease some of our parish finances."

"So, I welcome you all and turn your fortunes over now to Tracy Metzger, our new Iowa friend, who brings years of experience in running a Bingo hall. Take it away, Tracy!"

"That you, Father Eggert! Hallo Woodland Park! Hallo St. Mark's! Hallo all you folks coming in out of the cold! Gonna warm your hearts with easy money, a little gossip, and some coffee, sandwiches and treats from *ZigZag*, the best source of burgers in all the Great Lakes."

He rolled the cage, and Bingo balls began colliding and bouncing off one another. Each carried a letter and a number, fixed data that comforted Metzger, and he chuckled. These people were going to love Bingo...and he was going to love working for the diocese. He glanced around the hall...identified the Sikhs, caught the orange color of Geraldine's hair, saw Devlin chatting with a couple of fellows. Felt like he knew his crowd. Warm feelings everywhere. As promised.

Now, looking out over the hall, Metzger whetted appetites, "Are we ready to roll the odds, my friends?"

"Enough chatter, Tracy," came a voice, "Call the numbers!"

"Ya, ya...that's the way to say o.k. up here isn't it?" he laughed.

He paused, looked about the hall, smiled a confident grin...warm, welcoming, innocent. He said something about Criss Cross Burgers and moved into a reminiscence.

"Let me begin by sharing an old story about my late residence in Iowa...something I learned there." He paused. The crowd waited, a still silence.

"You all know that the Mississippi River begins here in Minnesota, right?"

"YESSSSSSS."

"But do you know why it flows so directly south into Iowa?"

"NOOOOOO."

"Well," he paused, "It's because Iowa sucks."

A brief silence and then a roar from the hall, and in the midst of the hilarity, Tracy Metzger spun the cage, reached in and pulled out the first number of the night: N-33.

LAW AND ORDER

O-67

A hulk carrying a career on his shoulders, an obstinate dedication in his heart, and wearying memories in his soul. His sweat protects the innocent. His thoughts create the illusion of insight. He has both walked the sidewalks offering security and stood in hallways reporting death. Devastating loss. Unaccountable loss. Delivering it sapped his soul, undermined resolve...and yet he continued. Homicide. The poison dart of crime. Always strikes the bulls-eye. Posture. Presentation. Presence. It is he.

Devlin took an extra breath, paused at the foot of the station's staircase. Icy. Sanded.

"Well," he said to no one in particular, "Someone was working this evening." He grabbed the rail and stepped up until he reached the landing. Paused, took a deep breath to prepare for his shift and heard a distant, high-pitched screech, something like a piece of metal being tortured into an unnatural mold...one note, one pitch. He listened for more. Silence.

He took his hat off and ran his forearm across his sweaty brow. Again, a listen. Still, the silence. Hmmm. Maybe a squeaky gate that didn't want to move. His skull cooled

11

quickly, and he grabbed the handle, pulled with a grunt and opened the large door. Hit a wall of heat. He paused. Removed his coat and gloves, nodded to Oswald the Desk Sergeant and moved down the corridor to his office. Paused and enjoyed the signage on his door: *Detective Lieutenant Chester Devlin, Woodland Park Police.*

He moved his bulk gracefully over to his desk and sat his considerable backside onto the cushioned rocker. "Aahhhhhhh," he sighed. Looked down at his desk and picked up the *Daily Report*. Sorted through the list. Not much to get excited about: shoplifting at *Marge's Fabric Shop*; two fights at Bockrath's bar; stolen keg of beer at *the Eagles Nest*. That was it. Pretty quiet. His shift would end somewhere near midnight. Decided to walk over to St. Mark's and see who showed up for a night of soft-core gambling.

Bingo. Kind of a silly game. Just sit there, listen to numbers being called and hope that Lady Luck dropped onto your shoulder. Winners always shouted as though they had accomplished something. Nah. Simply put, Lady Luck found them. That was all. He shrugged.

He spent a few minutes mulling over staffing issues, pulled himself out from behind his desk and called to Oswald, "Off to Bingo...later." Put on his coat, hat and gloves, walked out the door and gently found the sidewalk. Shoveled and sanded. Good. He turned and headed over to the Church Hall, passed by the entry to St. Mark's, continued to the end of the block and turned right. A dozen paces and he stepped up and in.

Swirling sounds welcomed him from behind closed doors, smacked him when he walked into the hall. He looked around for faces: Ole Jacobson; Per Olson, Father Harry

Eggert, and over to the left, Geraldine, seated alongside Sharon Cunningham. He looked further to the right and found Sylvia Ingram, and surprisingly, Ahmed Hassam. Didn't think Sikhs gambled...maybe a good-will visit. Well, they had a place in Woodland Park now.

He remembered when Muslim families from St. Paul tried to build a mosque. They made quite a bit of noise about needing tax-free property, and City Council reacted by quietly refusing to put the item on its agenda.

But the Sikhs had asked for nothing, simply moved into some older housing on the edge of the town and began living their lives. They were good neighbors. He liked seeing Ahmed out there in the gathering, fitting in. On impulse, he looked specifically for Jonas Kirk. Hadn't seen him around for many months...but he travelled a lot. Thought he would be back in town for the Valentine Bike Race. Didn't show.

Been what...a year? Devlin wondered what in the hell Kirk was doing. Not that he missed him...well maybe a little. He did find his little quips amusing, and he usually picked up the tab for a meal. Still, crime was their shared interest, especially homicide, and Woodland Park had been mercifully free of murder for more than a year and a half.

He added Kirk's absence to his memory calendar. Gone since last March maybe, and now winter's nearly over. Hmmm. Well, he was probably travelling, and he'd have a good story or two when he returned.

"Hey there, Devlin!"

He turned and returned the shout from Ole Jacobson, "Ya, ya, Ole! You gonna bring everyone donuts tonight? Got some money down on the table...find a home for your spare cash?" he laughed.

"I'm a winner don'cha know...and you look like a lost cause...buy some cards, see what Lady Luck can offer you tonight."

Devlin laughed, drew closer, "Think I will. I guess I can call it patrolling, keeping an eye on this crowd 'til I go off shift at midnight. What happens after that I guess is in the hands of the Gods."

"Whaddya mean?" Ole asked in a lower voice.

"Hell," Devlin whispered, "City Council is so short of funds the Department has to rotate the graveyard shift, but sometimes no one is available...overtime is limited. Like tonight for example, the streets will be empty after midnight. No cops out there...none at all."

"Yumpin Yiminy! All we need now is some break-in at 3:00 am and the whole town will be screaming about it... probably looking to blame you and your patrols, don'cha know."

"You got that right," Devlin replied, "Let's just hope that we can keep everyone guessin', especially the crooks. Hey, here comes Tracy Metzger. Ready to call his balls," Devlin laughed.

"Yeah," Ole smiled, "Bet he likes handling them too."

"Find a seat," Devlin laughed, "Sit your ass down and hope that you find some Bingo money to spend on the Vikings next season."

"Ya, Ya," he smiled as he sat. Devlin found a seat next to two old men on his left and two widows on his right. The men nodded to him, the women giggled. He ignored them, focused on his cards.

Tracy Metzger told a joke about the Mississippi River and pulled out the first ball of the evening: **N-33.**

WORSHIP
G-48

God is great! The cry went up from the sands of Arabia to the walls of Jerusalem. It echoed throughout the Tigris-Euphrates valley, reached India. It touched upon the boundaries of the Rhine, bounced off Moscow, found its way to India, rebounded to England, travelled to America. A people in need. A search to find ways to bear suffering, embrace a future. Death, the pathway to eternal life. God is great!

Ahmed Hassan walked slowly down the stairs to the praying space, each step a footfall of failure, reminders of his futile effort to create the sanctuary his followers needed. Punjab, India was a long way from this land of many lakes, he mussed, but we have come in good faith, and we are now a part of Woodland Park.

He allowed himself a small smile as he remembered the early days in St. Paul. One could walk any reasonable distance and pass the full spectrum of race, culture, nationality. But being present did not mean being seen. Sikhs were called Muslims and neither were welcome, even by those who lived the code of "Minnesota Nice".

He worked hard to distinguish his people, who wore a turban, from Muslims, who did not, an explanation that had little to do with doctrine or faith, but it kept a minority group distinctive...and safe. No need to distinguish their beliefs from those of the Hindu from whom they came. Reincarnation, yes. Caste system, no.

Inside the gurdwara, he had more serious challenges. Young people increasingly avoided praying with elders. Life in the city exposed them to different music, bizarre hair styles, tattoos, even sloppy clothing. When they walked into prayer meetings, they were criticized, ridiculed, driven away. New generation, new ways.

Nor did their "temple", as outsiders called it, provide separate worship venues for men and woman. Women wanted their own prayer space. Men felt both abused and ignored. Without a new gurdwara, how to resolve this tension? From what base could they practice their beliefs, school their children, mingle with the community? Were they becoming a threat to social stability? Sikhs were peaceful in heart, but fierce combatants, he grimaced to himself. Few outsiders knew that they carried a small dagger in their turbans, as required by their beliefs. Peaceful in manners; violent in conflict. Were they losing control? Hassan thought not, but he felt the time of gentle stirring was nearing an end.

More than once, members had pointed to Woodland Park as a likely location for their temple. Property values were relatively stable and affordable, and Ahmed could not argue with its general sense of inclusion. He'd been looking for the right building site for over a year, and lately he felt a more welcoming attitude. He wondered if he would see any young Sikhs at a gambling hall. Bingo, a gambit to take people's money. A game of chance. Forbidden. Still, maybe he should be seen there...a friendly gesture.

He asked Akar Singh to go with him over to St. Mark's. Always safer to travel in pairs. As they left their wooden, roughly painted house, they both paused, hearing a brief, high pitched scream, something like a hawk might make when calling, or maybe a target's last syllable of terror as it found itself in the grasp of those unyielding claws. They looked at one another...listened again...heard nothing more, each dismissing the sound with a nod...a piece of nature at work. They got in Singh's car, arrived at St. Mark's in time to survey the crowd before Tracy Metzger began calling out the numbers.

Ahmed hesitated as he approached the front doors. Maybe he should read how it went tomorrow in the *Gazette*. He paused, but Akar urged him on with quiet little motions. They opened the door slightly, enough to catch the din of conversation, murmurs of luck and hope, easily feeling the warming baritone of Tracy Metzger quipping with some pre-call chatter.

Glancing at one another, they moved quietly to the edge of the room, waited for the calls to begin. Ahmed took note of Geraldine Wright...now there was a piece of work...a gossip to circulate every rumor that hit the streets. And next to her, Sharon Cunningham. Gentle woman. Well-connected to the community, she knew property values. Noticed Chester Devlin come in, begin chatting with Ole Jacobson. Surprising. Didn't think he would like something this static.

Devlin noted the turbans along the side of the hall, wondered to himself what they were doing, showing up and then just watching. Friendly or judgmental? Other eyes also gave them a look, gazes as fixed in curiosity as they were hasty in judgment.

Metzger saw them settle into their side chairs, decided to set aside his joke about the pig who prayed five times a day that a Muslim would make it a pet. Mentioned Criss Cross sandwiches instead, then settled for an easier theme, the Mississippi River

"...because Iowa sucks!"

Brought the house down, he thought, and just what he wanted.

"Allll right, y'all gonna settle down now and let me get on to making some winners." First number of the night: N-33

BURGERS

B-10

Hunger. The human condition. Where to ease it? How to find a daily remedy? What price its possession? Some are simple consumers. Others work to satisfy the community's daily search for calories. There is honor in that. There is profit. There is danger. More than one provider feels the slice of competition. Difficult course. Praise to the survivor. Praise the Lord.

Fred Daggert paused. Looked again at the laptop and the spreadsheet for his two restaurants. Fast food remained in fashion, and he took some comfort that his receipts were keeping him above water...but just. The thought occurred that he needed to place another outlet in Woodland Park, but as before, the idea ran up against a firm reality. Cash reserves. He and Gordo drew on a solid core of savings to get bank financing for the first two *ZigZags*. But to expand further, he had to prove he could service a loan extension. Right now, he couldn't.

He had two parcels of land which might serve him well, but it would be a couple of years before he could think about expanding with either one. Still, he had made a bit of a name for himself...people talked about *ZigZag* with increased familiarity, "Good burgers...great service". He sighed. Just needed to keep building reputation.

Well, time to make the circuit, pick up the day's cash and drop it off at the bank. His managers would be a little surprised that he was coming by so early, but that was fine. Didn't like to have a schedule...kept people on their toes and helped him feel secure toting cash to the bank for night deposit.

With some satisfaction, he closed his laptop and gathered up his gloves and coat. He'd pick up Gordo and get on over to St. Mark's Hall and check on the food set-up.

He mussed again over his friend and partner. Gordo learned to march and operate heavy machinery in the Army, while he majored in business at St. Cloud State. He learned that no theory seemed to be worth a damn if a lot of common sense and suspicion didn't protect a successful cash flow. Graduating, he moved through a series of entry level jobs. Wasn't fun but he learned a lot about key aspects of operating a successful business...minimum income, inventory control, quality standards, financing and cash flow, site management, worker relations. Easy words to think about, he said to himself, but they covered a hell of a lot of trouble.

Finally decided he wanted his own company. First step...financing. Three years after leaving St. Cloud, he connected again with Gordo now back from service and fortified with a wad of cash he had saved from rank pay and gambling. Fred had $25 thousand. Gordo matched it, and together they opened their first *ZigZag.* Burgers, accessible and tasty, satisfied both hunger and edginess.

Fast food was a proven market and the challenge was clear enough. Make a better burger. They did. Catering improved the bottom line too, but he still needed a greater market share in Woodland Park. Somehow, somewhere, he had to find money to build the business. Needed to think outside the box.

He grunted with some satisfaction that he had outbid McDonald's and Arby's for the rights to provide food and drink to the Bingo crowd. Gave him a chance to get his product in front of some movers and shakers, even if he had to find more staff. A few applicants happily named Tracy Metzger as their reference and Daggert hired them right away. Well worth it. Gordo reported that they knew their business and showed a lot of personality. Still, where was he gonna find the extra cash he needed to expand the franchise?

ZigZag. Great name. He laughed. Who knew what direction his business was headed...so long as it was growing, he felt good. Opened the door of his office to step outside. Cold but not snowing and he liked that...built appetites. Checked the doorknob...locked.

As he turned to get into his car, he heard a screech, distant, but not what he thought of as a predator's success. He listened harder. The night reclaimed the silence. Hmmm. He stood perfectly still...all quiet. Shrugged his shoulders, opened the car door and climbed in. Turned the ignition and felt good about the immediate response from the engine. Not a nice night to be stranded. Go by the bank, pick up Gordo and head over to St. Mark's.

Ten minutes after he dropped his deposit, snow began to fall. He slowed down, parked and hit the horn. Three times. Gordo finally showed his face. Looked at the snow, went back in and came out in boots and stocking cap. He settled into his cold, leather seat and looked over at Fred, "Are you sure this is where you want to spend the evening?"

"Yep. We got six staff over there managing sandwiches, snacks and drinks and I wanna be sure that they are doing it right. Always good to provide a bit of back-up on an opening night."

"Yea...you're right. Hate the snow...looks like its gonna stick...heard any weather prediction?"

"Talked about 8-10 inches by morning."

"That means snow shovels."

"Worse. Means plows for both locations... you cover Parrot St. and I'll get the other one eh?"

"Yeah...I can do that."

"Hell, look at that...the hall must be full, no parking on the streets or the side lot...gonna have to go around back near the food van."

"Damn," Gordo commented as they turned the corner, "It's really gonna snow...what a mess."

They parked, spent time with the staff, satisfied themselves that sales were going smoothly and walked into the back of the hall just as Tracy Metzger got ready to start pulling out Bingo Balls. He noticed them, changed his patter, "O.K., folks, an early special for tonight, compliments of *Zig-Zag*...and you like their food cause you're eating it almost as fast as I can call a number. Nod to Fred Daggert and Gordo there. Thanks, guys."

Tracy turned to the crowd, "Winner of our first game gets a free Criss Cross Burger each day for a week. Wash it down with a free drink too!"

"It's snowing outside, Tracy!" a voice called out. "Warm us up!"

"Yeah, yeah, I'll add free coffee, o.k.?" Metzger smiled, told a joke about the Mississippi River. Lots of laughs. Then, he grabbed a ball, "Here we go: N-33."

TEN AND OUT

I-28

In clouds they form. To earth they fall. Flakes, white and wet, insulating animal runs and caves, concealing that which might cause alarm, creating forms seldom seen by the ordinary eye. Hide from the freeze. Seek warmth. Huddle in mirth. Some nights, nature wins...and men lose.

On it came. Ten inches of sloppy, wet paste began filling foundation cracks and windshields. Crusty ice soon covered the slosh, leaving roofs a little creaky, turning outdoor stairs into slippery hip-breakers. Blended, manicured yards became platters of white with no edge in sight. Cursing the gods, homeowners got out their shovels and businesses called in plows as both began their losing fight against heavy, blowing snow.

Behind *Stone Cold Charity* irregular mounds of off-hour donations slowly became white-capped moguls. Plastic bags crinkled, cracked. Torn fabrics in three sofas and two chairs rippled into fixed waves, shielding crickets and mice who had sorted themselves into impromptu shelters. A sneaky wind began to wind its way around the corners of Woodland Park, racing through the alley and piling snow firmly against its walls.

A few blocks away, a warm, buoyant crowd of well-fed gamblers kept scanning their Bingo cards, hoping to win the next one, gossiping openly about neighbors, friends and public officials. At the breaks, they whispered news of local love affairs, deceptive dollar movements and corrupt business rivals. Not much surfaced about religious tolerance or theological principles. No need. As Tracy Metzger called the numbers, good fortune visited Lutherans, Catholics and non-believers alike. Along the sides of the hall a few Sikhs sat, observing and encouraging the fun while two known Muslim religious leaders chatted, ate devilled-egg sandwiches and sipped soft drinks.

Every run of the numbers brought moans, cheers and catcalls as cash spread itself over the crowd. Surreptitious sips of alcohol kept brandy lovers in warm conversations, and the entire hall oooohed when Metzger offered a surprise game to finish the evening.

"I gotta say," he began, "I've been doing this Bingo routine for almost ten years...different parts of Iowa, an early start in Pennsylvania and now this warm, rowdy bunch in Woodland Park."

He paused, waiting for the crowd to quiet and give him a listen. It did, and he hurried on, "First, a report. I received a note telling me that this is prom night in Iowa. I wondered how anyone would know that and asked for more information. Report says that there were ten tractors at every McDonald's."

Loud, raucous laughter, many jeers and hilarious images of high schoolers sorting through harvesters and hamburgers. Metzger let the crowd have its way then said solemnly:

"For this last game of the evening, we're offering a special prize: $500!"

The room became very quiet.

"That's right, $500 and I'm not kidding...buy a lot of groceries or a couple of cases of brandy, eh?"

Laughter. Focused attention.

"But of course, there's a catch."

Moans, a catcall.

Metzger let silence take control, then went on.

"So, this is the deal. I will be drawing only 10 balls. If we have a **BINGO**, the winner or winners will take or divide $500."

Cheers throughout the hall. "Roll it! Let 'er go, Tracy!"

Metzger let it build.

Geraldine shouted, "Dammit, let's have it, Tracy!"

Metzger rolled the basket and with appropriate seriousness, pulled out the ten balls:

N-33; B-5; I-23; O-75; B-53. "Oh, sorry folks, misread it. Should be G-53." Metzger then continued: N-41; I-16, O-68, I-19.

He paused...folks still looking for that last winning number...silence.

G-46

Scurrying looks, gasps, then a room full of "oh, my, none of my numbers...well, pretty good evening...lotta fun... that last one, I was so close."

Metzger laughed and thanked everyone for coming out. "Take your winnings and help a soul less fortunate, folks... tell your friends, and we'll be back here next week for another run at the easy money."

With moans and a few cheers, the crowd dispersed. Some went back to the *ZigZag* counter for an evening snack. Most went out through the front doors, and that let the cold swoop in, a sobering, settling change of temperature. Out came coats, hats and gloves.

"Well, that was a pretty tidy wrap up to the evening," Sharon Cunningham commented to Geraldine, "I think I'll come back next week...lot of fun seeing people just unwind a bit...nice and comfortable in here, and I'm thinking winter is going to take a good bite out of us this week."

"Glad you liked it, Sharon, but by God, I'm not so happy. Spent nearly $50 bucks one way or another and won nothing...I caught a look at Chester and he wasn't very happy either. But damn, he should be. He doesn't have to work the graveyard shift."

"Oh...so who covers the town tonight?"

"Hell, there's no one out there between midnight and 6:00 am. Just don't have the staffing...that's a secret... don't spread it."

"Oooh! Does Chester pull that duty sometimes, Deeni?"

"No, but he feels he has to show his face when there aren't any cops in the streets. He's really sort of dear that way...lots of noise from him, I know, but inside, he's really committed to protecting the town."

"Well, I doubt anyone's gonna be busting into anything tonight...my bet is that we're gonna see a big, winter dump out there. Get your boots on. I'll give you a ride home."

Two steps out of the Bingo Hall and they were in six inches of snow. They mushed to Sharon's car.

"What a load of white crap," Geraldine commented, "A hard wind'll freeze everything to stone...dammit, Sharon, watch your step or I'll have to drive."

HANGOVER

N-44

White. Dilutes landscape and faces. Conceals both the innocence of social change with the calculation of self-interest. Simple in presentation. Complicated in its absorption of pattern. Reach outside the frame and suck into the picture that which is new, incongruous, ravenous, deadly. Now all is singular. Hidden. Blended. Spotless. Pure. White.

The Bishop dreamed. Images both soft and hard moved with a blur through his mind and wound about. There! The figure, shrouded and black, formed from nothing, creating substance out of thought. A man! He moved quietly, far more smoothly than one might anticipate given his apparent age. He slipped from the car he had parked out of the scene, his voice echoing that he would return, walked toward the entry, passed it by and went around to the alley. Always someone there looking for shelter. Found his target, as he hoped he would. The figure reached inside his cloak.

He gripped the blade--dark, sharp, long and lethal, approached the lone figure leaning up against the concrete wall, searching in the discarded clothing bags for something to layer up and keep warm. He looked around as the tall figure approached him, saw his eyes, knew their threat and turned to go. "No harm, man...just wanna stay warm...not gonna hurt anyone...not stealing... just trying to find a little..." and then the movement of the knife, buried in a single motion.

The man's cry shattered the quiet, moved out of the alley and cast itself in a bubble of sound that carried over several blocks. To many listeners, it became the distant cry of a successful predator. But for the swirling image, it was a sound that caused his cloak to flare. He dissolved momentarily, then formed again, watching.

As the man fell, his fingers reached out for help that would not arrive, grabbed cloth from the shadowy figure, tore a segment away and wrapped it in his hand, even as he lost his grip on life.

The standing figure shed his cloak and it disappeared. His silhouette wiped the knife off in the clothes of its victim, concealed it in his own. He bent over and stuffed a note into the slumping man's shirt.

Ambitions, fortified by stealth and the cloak of night, now bloomed. Head held high, the figure appeared suddenly at the front door, entered and found privacy. Floated quietly out of the shop to his car. Got in and made a brief comment to his passenger, she still staring at passing headlights. He started the car and gently pulled into the street. A few minutes later, the snow began to fall, filling the alley with layered insulation.

There, a homeless, nameless, lifeless body cooled, hardened, sank into the anonymity of white art. Blood, at first congealed, now hardened into a concealed red skating surface and the ragged clothes that covered his knife wound set themselves into the chaotic placement found in his fall. Death resided. Irrevocable. Unnoticeable. White.

Burkey jerked awake, sweating. Terrible night! Frightening dreams! His mind stirred slowly, wandered a bit, then centered. Still lying in bed, he sorted through the cluttered margins between mists and reality. Needed to clear his mind. He turned on his radio and waited for morning news...lots of chatter about snow and temperatures, but he wanted something else. Early segments talked of the new Bingo night at St. Mark's, and he grumbled his approval. Still, nothing seemed to satisfy him. Where were the reporters covering the streets, the police station, the talk about City Council? Where was the news?

He switched stations.

"...and on that note, we leave you with hopes for an early melt and a fear that there may be sad discoveries under the snow. A Big Freeze is settling in and it may be a week before we'll find out what is buried in the white ice, right Roxie?"

"Right back at'cha, Mike. Doubt that an ice pick would get me down to the mound of manure I set out last fall... it'll be there come spring, but right now, it's part of an ice cake. Gonna be awhile...well, 'nough of that, Mike. Whaddya say we wring a little humor out of a lousy scene outside?

"Ya, ya, that's what Ole said to me yesterday."

"What Mike? What did Ole say?"

He said, "When it snows, pray for rain."

"Ole is a fool," Roxie smiled through the mike, *"Only reason he wants rain is that people will be afraid to step outside his café...they'll spend all day sippin' coffee and munching donuts."*

"Maybe that would fill up Ole's Donut 'Ole," Mike laughed a bit.

"I'm thinking maybe he should break crumbs from day old pastry and create little trails around town that would lead people to his shop...you know...a Hansel/Gretel gambit."

"Really, Roxie...crumbs for the bums kind of thing?"

"Well, people like treats...even those that are for the birds."

"Stunning strategy, Roxie...but were gonna have a Big Melt in another 10 days or so and then, guess what?"

"I'm hungry for a secret, Mike, so what is it...maybe we'll find my lost shovel?"

"More than that, Rox...my guess is that we'll find a lot of garbage and probably a few cats and maybe a dog or two locked in ice...sad, but just part of good living in Woodland Park. Got to take the bad with the good."

"You take it, Mike, I'll settle for just the good...ooops time is up...we gotta get out of here..."

"Ya. Ya. Stick around all you people of Woodland Park. We'll have more at mid-day on the whiteout. This is Michael Conway sending you back to Morning Notes with Rolf and Ray.

"This is Roxie Rochambeau complaining that Mikie is shutting me down. Boo to you, Mike...and bye, bye for now."

Burkey cleared his throat, continued his rotation through the major news stations, found nothing to hold his interest and headed to the shower. Picked up his daily discarded clothing...had a thought or two about it, then shrugged and put it into the laundry. Maid would be washing later that day.

He showered. Easier to cleanse the body than the soul. Pondered again the forces he had set in motion. A conservative Catholic cleric by nature, he had found the recent change in tone by Pope Francis a difficult challenge to digest. Easy enough to speak of embracing fellow men, honoring all souls, uplifting the poor, but the Pope didn't have to deal with falling income and the Muslim encroachment into his diocese. He scrubbed his skin briskly, cleaning out pores and tainted cells of every kind.

Why speak of Muslims as being God's children when they were filling in housing units, their numbers eating into the faith base of the community. Reduced attendance at St. Mark's was no longer just a quirk. It was a harbinger, and he saw no future for himself as leader of an evaporating Catholicism. Father Eggert was an excellent parish priest, but the diocese needed additional leadership. Rome wouldn't pay for it, and he couldn't afford it. Tiresome. At one point a couple of years ago, he thought that he might be elevated to Archbishop and assigned to the Vatican. But nothing came of it. Completely devastating. He scrubbed harder.

Now this invasion.

Muslims were a problem. They multiplied in ways that Catholics used to. Disciplined in their faith, focused on their families, they improved both the economic and moral tone of the community. Yet he did not want to share space with them. Far better they be kept outside Woodland Park. Let them go north to St. Cloud where they seemed to be welcomed. His brush began to leave small traces of blood on his skin.

Well, he had a response ready for the "infidels". He smiled as he said that. He, not they, would determine the faith base of Woodland Park. He felt good about his plan. No public attack...sure to backfire...but if he could frighten the community, that would be enough. Irrational worry carried its own energy, found its own outlet. Give Woodland Park a Muslim target and hostility would blanket them and the Sikhs.

He smiled to himself. When might the storm pass and release the religious contagion he had set in motion? Soon, but not today. It was risky...perhaps the greatest chance of his religious life...but as he thought about it, probably a necessary one. When news of the killing emerged, he would have to play it carefully.

He would send out his monthly message to parishioners, expressing deep concern for the homeless, his concern about the social dynamic of a Muslim minority. Encourage caution, identify fear, find its focus...let rejection flow. He finished scrubbing, small flecks of blood on his arms, little smears flowing with the water.

Would be helpful if he could court that dunce of a cop, Devlin. Never will quite get over the way he insulted him during the inquiries about the knifing death in St. Marks. Of course, Jonas Kirk had been a little more thoughtful... even if his logic had the slight stench of betrayal about it.

At least Father Eggert remained in the cop loop. Last week Devlin mentioned to him that he planned to attend Bingo to show a police presence on nights when there was no graveyard shift. Eggert in turn reported the whole little scenario to Burkey, and the Bishop conveyed it to Tracy Metzger. Safe hall. Empty streets. Snow and cold outside, warmth inside.

His thoughts complete for the moment, he left the shower, dried his body, carefully cleaning his fingernails. Threw the lightly blood -stained towel into the hamper. He put on an informal, white gown that he could wear anywhere. Always want to appear to be in command...always.

Two things to do today. Call Alice Goodwin. See if she remembered anything odd about last night. Compliment her for working so closely with *Stone Cold Charity*. Her commitment raised the Church's visibility among the needy...made it more important to the public...and it kept Alice focused more on herself, less on what he was doing.

He smiled to himself...it was a little awkward last night, dropping off some used clothing, discussing the poor with *Charity* director, Victoria Blessing while he was dressed in his formal vestments. But he had to make his way directly over to St. Marks to bless the first night of Bingo and offer some encouraging words. Best to look impressive. Well-dressed. Sign of good leadership, and as it turned out, he was well equipped for the evening.

Victoria never seemed to notice his style of dress. She seemed much more focused on what he was saying. Timely too that he could just wander a bit, take in her line of products, then leave a little after closing time. Got Alice seated in the car, then excused himself for a moment...needed to use the rest room. Patted his sash for reassurance, took a few minutes, then drove Alice over to the Bingo hall. He was a little late, but all in all, quite tidy, if he did say so himself.

Burkey cleared his throat...well, best to see how it went last night. Father Eggert seemed enthusiastic about the crowd and if attendance held up, there might be a real treasure to be discovered there. And that Tracy Metzger. Hard to believe he was willing to come all the way up from Cedar Rapids, but then again, Burkey knew Metzger's game. Now, he needed to confirm that everything had gone well. Clever code...hope it worked.

Freshly groomed. Nicely postured. Fully satisfied. Burkey opened the bottom of his crozier and removed the knife. Grabbed his beads and prayer book, headed on downtown. Took a side turn to drive over the Canal Bridge. Open water. Gave the knife a fling. Gone. God's work be done. Praise the Lord!

DEVLIN

O 64

Safety. The foundation of a stable community.

As snow fell and cold set its form, a small van equipped with chains pushed its way across Woodland Park, cautiously slowing at intersections, turning finally into Woodland Bank where it parked for well over a quarter of an hour. When the clock ticked 2:00 a.m., its side door opened, seamlessly.

Three figures emerged, two carrying equipment. They stopped next to the night depository, opened the bin door and with a compact, hydraulic tool, wrenched it off its hinges and set it aside in the snow. They sent a cable with a large, gripping claw into the drop box.

One last look about, and they reeled up bags of cash and deposit slips, a total of six late night drops by Woodland Park merchants. Total time elapsed: eight minutes.

They took their packages and equipment in arms, retreated to the van, closed the doors, creating a puff of exhaled air that carried with it a ZigZag wrapper. In the dark silence of the night they drove away, quietly making all the correct signals, steadily finding their way out of Woodland Park. Not a policeman in sight. Not a patrol car moving. Empty streets.

Outlined in a hint of dawn, Detective Lieutenant Chester Devlin lurched through the snow cursing the cold, wishing to God that he had managed a better night of sleep. Last night's Bingo was boring...the incessant call of numbers, the eclectic gasps of discovery, an occasional shout of success. All so predictable in a mass audience and St. Mark's Hall was *stuffed* with people and empty bellies. *ZigZag* must have sold out. Burgers. He could savor the flavor even now.

But it was early morning following what the department had begun to call a Dark Night. And after that empty graveyard shift someone had to staff early hours. Today, his turn. Duty.

Snow still falling and temperatures plummeting...not likely to be anyone out and about...for good or for ill. He reached the front doors of the station, stomped his feet a couple of times in a show of some sort of courtesy and pulled the handle.

He stepped right through a curtain of warm air into a dimly lit space and crossed hardwood floors sealed with a sheen of dirt baked by a hundred thousand footfalls. No echo whatsoever. He shed his coat and gloves, walked into the operations room, noted that Oswald was on break once again and glanced over to the action board. Nothing.

Well, that's the way it should be. Quiet night, bad weather, no time for crazies or drunks lurching about the streets. A boring morning. He reflected on his mood...calm and thoughtful. Everything about Woodland Park seemed to suit him lately. Lots of little whines from merchants about loitering and littering, but citations had been confined to a few DUI, some occasional flying fists, a car crash or two... nothing really engaging. Quite comfortable.

He poured himself a coffee, carried it into his office, looked over the duty roster for the next two weeks. Noted another Dark Night in five days, followed by another just three days later. Irregular patterns for sure, he thought, but a short-handed staff demanded unpredictability.

The phone rang. No one answered, and he looked over at Oswald's desk...not back yet from wherever. Devlin leveraged himself up out of his chair, walked with a rocking footfall over to the counter and picked up the phone. And now his day began.

"HELLO! HELLO! POLICE! we've been robbed...night deposit, cash, receipts, everything they could get...GONE! GONE! Get over here, NOW!"

Devlin heard the shout, and tingles ran right along his arm. He gripped the phone, "PERCY! PERCY! Is that you? What the hell is going on over there?"

"DEVLIN! Get over here...we've been robbed...dammit, we've been robbed!"

"I'm on my way, Percy! Don't touch a thing."

Devlin grabbed his coat and gloves, felt for his pistol and headed out the door. A dozen steps and he was in his patrol car, slamming the door, revving the engine, turning hard, sliding. "Ooops," he thought, "No time to play keystone cops." He slowed, cautioned by slick surfaces and falling snow. Hard morning to be moving about. Damn, damn, damn...a bank robbery. He murmured to himself, "What the hell is this all about?"

Took him a good ten minutes to get over to the bank, park and get inside where he found President Percy Whitcomb, a good friend.

"O.K., Percy, whatta ya know?"

"I know that the Night Depository has been raided, Chester. Cover door wrenched off, some kind of device sucked or lifted the deposit bags up out of their bin...and then nothing."

"Got any signs. Foot traffic or car tracks?"

"Let me show you," and he walked Devlin outside. "Look at this snow...hell, it's been falling for a good twelve hours, and right now anything down near the street is covered in a good 8-10 inches of that white stuff."

"Got any idea whose deposits were taken...any regulars?"

"Well, ordinarily I get bags from *Ole's Donut 'Ole* and from *ZigZag* ...sometimes from *Rudy's Grocery*...but hell, I don't know. Whatever was in there is gone, 'cept for a *ZigZag* wrapper plastered up against the edge of the building."

Percy pointed toward the depository. "Guess Fred was careless when he dropped the deposits into the bin. But that's it. I'll be waiting to hear from a half-dozen businesses once the word gets out...and I'm guessing we're talking about a good $15-20 thousand...most of it in cash."

"O.K. Got it. We'll get some lab people out here...dust for prints, see if they can find any traces of a vehicle...what about a security camera...where is it?"

"It's right up there where it should be," Whitcomb pointed, "But it's covered in sleet and snow...doubt that it's gonna be of much help. Might have had a chance if there were some patrol last night...might have seen something before snow covered everything...anyone circling the town last night, Chester?"

"Nope. Sorry Percy. Was one of those Black Nights, no patrol between midnight and six a.m. That's gotta change, but until the City Council can do something about our budget, we really don't have much choice. Just a bit of bad luck, I guess."

"Ya! Ya! Ya! Bad luck you say, Chester, but chances of finding stolen cash are now slim to scanty panties. This security crap has got to get changed right away...who else is gonna find themselves robbed in the morning, eh? And when's the next blackout night for the cops, anyway?"

"Can't say, Percy. You know that. Word gets out, crime gets worse. It's just irregular, nothing that anyone could plan on...and I'm kinda surprised that they hit the bank... quite a gamble when no one knows when the patrols are cancelled."

"Gamble, crap, scramble...who knows...but damn it, Chester, this really can't happen again. When does City Council meet?"

"Two weeks, Percy, but you better do a little lobbying if you want anyone to take the situation seriously. People don't usually feel too sorry for banks."

"Don't give a damn, Chester! It's people's money and I gotta keep it safe. It'll take some cash, but this drop box will never be vulnerable again...damn it's cold. I'm goin' inside...want some coffee."

"Might as well...not much for me to do here and the station house is practically empty anyway. Apart from you, no crime reports, which I guess is a good thing."

"*Solving the robbery* would be a good thing, Chester... keep that in mind."

SHARON CUNNINGHAM

G 51

She appears to be ageless. Her body flows gracefully and with purpose. About her there is calm, thoughtful introspection. Within her there is sexual passion whetted by abstinence, anger fueled by dismissal. She speaks softly, thinks clearly, acts ruthlessly. She smooths social tensions, fuels admiration. She stores secrets even as she asks others to share theirs. Sharon Cunningham. She is an honorable woman. Touch her and you will remember that moment.

A week now and locals took to calling it the Great Bank Robbery. No suspects; no found cash; no arrested burglars...nothing. Chatter in *Ole's Donut 'Ole* ground away on it, but until the storm eased and melted a bit, there was not much to be found. The snow returned Saturday and Sunday followed by another wave of cold. Now it was Wednesday, Bingo night, and finally, a break. Temperatures rose into the 40s, winds calmed, the melt began and local chatter now speculated on what might be found under the frozen surface.

Sharon Cunningham made the trek over to Ole's alone, Geraldine deflecting an invitation in favor of spending time with Chester. Guess they were going to have a nice day of their own. That was fine. Sharon mused a bit about this business of living as a single woman. Since her return from India, now almost two years, she had managed to re-insert herself into Woodland Park, particularly into the business of St. Mark's. Felt good to be needed. Felt good to be home.

She didn't speak much about that time in the land of Hindu's and missionaries, happy enough to let people conclude that she finally had enough of time spent far, far away. But a few months after she returned, news of Father Lockhart's sudden death shocked the community. Its focus drifted back to Sharon. What could she tell? Had the good priest been ill at all? Had he made enemies in India? Any reports of any special assaults on Church property or its personnel?

Her comments remained general: "He never knew when to rest...He had been spending a lot of time flying to Rome...I think he was going to get an assignment there... His compassion for the poor never ebbed...It was an honor serving him and God."

But in the night, alone, she let her mind wander over her life with Father Lockhart...time begun right in the confessional booth at St. Mark's, moments concealed in Church visits to outlying parishes, the intimacy of serving God and man amidst the Hindu populations. Then, painfully, the gradual loss of the man, not the priest, but the man. Well, she had done her best to ensure the success of the mission, buying property upon which to build, serving as his personal representative in many social settings, speaking for him when he was gone to Rome.

But his ambition grew, his attention diminished, and she knew it was time to go…hard to do…difficult to say goodbye. She decided to return to Woodland Park, but on her own terms. He was in Rome. He returned, and she was gone. He said not a word, turned not a leaf to reclaim her…and then a few months later, he failed to appear at breakfast and upon examination, failed even to breathe.

Hard news for everyone: Alice Goodwin, Father Eggert, Geraldine Wright. Bishop Burkey seemed especially discouraged, likely she thought, because his name had begun to surface in the Vatican through the mouth of Father Lockhart. Burkey wanted to become Archbishop somewhere, maybe even assigned to Rome. Now, he was locked into a diocese which seemed to have very limited growth.

Even Jonas Kirk found Lockhart's death of interest. She remembered a conversation with him regarding things in India generally, and he had gentle questions about Father Lockhart, even made some inquiries of his own. Well, it was over…or should she say, to herself, "It was done".

That conclusion set her mind free on those evenings when she mentally revisited India, and then she slept. Still, she missed missionary work. She liked serving the poor. Providing shelter and food for those on the brink of starvation had warmed her. She had bonded with the generous spirit of the Hindu, found Muslims open, accommodating even, to her offers of support.

Now, back in Woodland Park, she reached out to Sikhs, finding their quiet, determined spirit of settlement familiar, and their connection to Hinduism comforting. It had been a Hindu, Saddhu Chakraborty, who had guided her to her comfortable acceptance of her relationship with Father Lockhart, who gave her a sense of her place on earth, allowing her to cultivate her respect for charity. When she learned of the Sikh search for a temple site, a gurdwara they called it, she went to their leader, Ahmed Hassan, offering to help. He seemed skeptical, but they chatted a bit, and he agreed that she might have helpful insight into the community.

Well, she sighed, she should get back to him on that. Took some small bites of her cream-filled donut. Sipped at her coffee. Decided to go to Bingo tonight. Good time last Wednesday and likely to continue. Fun to see people, especially Hassan. She knew neither Sikhs nor Muslims gambled and yet faces of both religions mingled with the crowd last week, offering to be a part of the community. Recognition might bring respect.

She let her thoughts dwell on Hassan. Quiet, erect, commanding beard and turban, he radiated a quiet competence. She could see why he had emerged as a leader for the Sikhs. He seemed to be unattached and that seemed peculiar. He, such a handsome man and she, increasingly lonely. Mentally, she flirted with him and liked the feeling it provoked. Maybe she could capture a little of his attention.

Now, how would that look, she smiled, a middle-aged carefully groomed white woman cavorting around Woodland Park in the company of a dark-skinned Sikh, uncut hair crowned with a well wrapped turban. She liked the idea.

She finished her coffee, said good-bye to Ole and walked down to *Large Marge's Fabrics*. Shopped the dress section, found a wrap that pleased her, green with yellow slashes, a short V neckline, tight waist and gently clinging skirt.

She took that home, napped, then bathed, shaved her legs, lightly perfumed the collar of her dress and wrapped the flowing fabric around her. Secured it in place with an angled waist cord that led the eye directly across her naval. Let's see how he reacts to this, she smiled.

A dull but active level of chatter greeted her as she opened the door of the Bingo Hall, stepped in and removed her coat. Carrying it lightly, she looked about for a friendly face and took a seat next to Alice Goodwin, Altar Society President and widely known admirer of Bishop Burkey.

"Good evening, Alice. Looks like a winning crowd out here again?"

"Hi Sharon! Oh, *a thinning crowd*...I don't think so...looks larger than last week. You want a drink?"

Sharon smiled to herself, positioned her face more directly to Alice's and repeated the message in different words, "Lot of people looking to be winners, eh Alice?"

"Oh, gosh yes, *they'll all be looking for dinners.* I was saying to Bishop Burkey earlier this week that *ZigZag* ought to expand the menu a bit, maybe lure people into staying around a while and eating a little more."

Sharon sighed, decided to go with Alice's line of talk.

"Well, Bishop Burkey certainly has been active in getting this Bingo going...heard that he reached out to Iowa to bring in this new fellow, Metzger...knew him personally."

"He must," Alice responded, "Cause I heard him in conversation with Tracy...I call him by his first name now...and he was saying that it was very important to get things done on time and keep the crowd engaged... no matter how he did it."

"Well, I think he has a winner there, Alice. Oh, I see Ahmed Hassan...think I'll have a quick chat with him before Metzger draws the first ball. Be right back."

"On your way, Sharon. I'll be here soaking up the gossip, even if it's two tables away," she smiled.

"I'll bet (*but I have my doubts*). Hold my seat." Sharon smiled, gently rose to go say hello to Hassan.

He saw her coming...how could he not? A jewel moving gracefully through a room full of quartz. She exuded charm, intelligence, a smile for everyone in general and an eye nicely fixed on him. Delightful woman, he thought, and awaited her arrival.

She nodded hello to a few of the fellows who hung out at Ole's, and in a seemingly wandering mode stopped almost abruptly, facing Ahmed, allowing the scent of perfume to flow on. He noticed.

"Good evening, Ahmed. It's very nice to see you here, but I'm sure that Bingo's not your favorite game, is it?"

"Ah, Sharon," he smiled with flashing white teeth complementing the color of the muted red turban he wore around his head. "I saw you when you came in the door and came to rest next to Alice Goodwin. She is a good woman, though sometimes a little dense...perhaps Bingo is exactly the game for her."

"Oh, Ahmed, you know better. She is just a little hard of hearing and sometimes conversation ends up going somewhere you don't expect. But she's very nice and does an excellent job looking after Bishop Burkey and he likes that kind of attention...might be useful if we ever need a favor from him, eh?"

"Who is the 'we' you speak of, Sharon?"

"Well," she laughed, "It might be you...or me...or we. Are you still interested in looking around for some property that would serve as a core temple...something you could build upon?"

"I am...we are. And you...still willing to help with our search?"

"I am indeed. Storm's supposed to break. We might be looking at some warmer temperatures later this week. Want to go looking about a bit on the weekend?"

"That would be a very fine moment for me," Hassan spoke gently. "Did you have any part of the town in mind?"

"Oh, not especially. Meet me at Ole's about 10 a.m. on Saturday, and I'll treat you to a bit of sweet something and some warm coffee. Then we'll go take a look at some properties."

"It shall be, Sharon," Ahmed responded. "Ah, look up now. Here is Tracy Metzger, ready to start the evening... winners all, eh?"

"Well, I think *we* are, Ahmed," she felt her temperature begin to rise. She smiled warmly, felt herself a little skittish inside. Time to take a break from him, she thought. "See you on Saturday, fun time."

Sharon moved back to her table seat next to Alice.

"Gonna win, Alice?" she asked.

"*Whatta din it is*, indeed, Sharon."

She didn't respond...savored some thoughts of Ahmed.

Tracy Metzger welcomed the crowd and spun the wire cage filled with balls.

"Say folks...here's a story:

Did you hear about the Iowa farmer who started the day wearing only one winter boot?

He heard there was a 50% chance of snow.

When the laughter calmed, Tracy turned to business.

"I see many winners out there...here we go!"

G 48!

BONDING

N 37

Feel the invisible force of attraction. Now found in the galaxy, and beyond, but equally powerful in the person and within. A look that carries packets of light from one set of eyes to another. Therein lies the bond. Innocence cannot provide immunity. Experience is no guide. One need not name it. It is. Two carriers of energy. They are vulnerable to life. To death.

Ten o'clock in the morning, the best moment of the day to be in *Ole's Donut 'Ole.* Crowd awake on coffee and sugar. Local news making the rounds in various forms. Coats off, legs stretched. A heated cave.

Sharon Cunningham wandered in, quietly searching for Hassan, finding him toward the back of the booths, joining him with a quiet hello and a smile.

"You are a picture of health on this bitter cold morning, Sharon," He began, smiling.

"Oh, Ahmed," she laughed, "Truth is a trick to spin, but I like the way you tell it."

"Then, may I say that your face reveals the joy of your nature and warms the room."

"You're going out on a limb, Ahmed...but a pliable one," she smiled.

"Coffee?"

"Please...and a small iced donut."

"It shall be done. I will return."

Even as he wandered to the front of the store, hailing Ole with an order, he thought to himself that Sharon Cunningham was a person of warmth and candor who invested her energy in good callings, especially for those who were in great need. In many ways, she represented all that he had hoped to find in the Woodland Park community...a generosity of spirit that accepted and admired the work of the Sikhs and welcomed Muslims.

Maybe today's meeting was a part of her social investment in people...then again, maybe she felt a little of the personal connection to him that he felt toward her. Best not to go too far with that line of thought...well here comes the coffee and the donut, Sharon. Let's see what we can work out together, one way or the other.

She watched him move across the room, up to the front... liked the way he kept his eyes forward, engaging Ole, speaking softly, his body language fluid, welcoming and appreciative of prompt service. That turban of his seemed to move as a rubber ball might bump and redirect through a room full of furniture. She liked the idea of being able to just glance and see where he was.

He placed the coffee carefully in front of her, rested the small plate with the donut beside it and sat down quietly. His mind absorbed her presence, a scent of some oil that he seemed to find familiar in his memories of India. She looked up...smiled.

"So, Hassan, what is it that you are trying to do here in Woodland Park?"

"Ah, Sharon. As you know from your time spent in India, Sikhs are distinct from Muslims, more akin to Hindus without caste, and our way of life is committed to building community, finding a place within it and of course being able to worship freely. Today, we find ourselves without a gurdwara, and we wish to find a placement."

"And I can help you how?"

"You are familiar with real estate properties in Woodland Park; you are also very active in supporting charitable distributions, and my sources tell me that *Stone Cold Charity* is looking for a new home, one closer to the growing edges of new housing and the business district in general."

"I hear the same things, Hassan, and so what interest have you in that decision?"

"I would like to have your opinion on the suitability of that small building they occupy...whether it might form the core of an expanded space which we could rebuild and expand into our temple."

"Hmmmm. I could see how that might be of interest. You'd still be part of the community, but not directly in it...not pressing your activities and worship into the residential heart...not threatening. And it is a nice sound building. Needs some updating I'm sure. It might be a little small, though the land about it would be quite adequate...want to go out there and have a look."

"I would, Sharon. Let's finish coffee and take a drive...be done before lunch would you say?"

"Oh, yes, I would think so."

Twenty minutes later they managed to find a freshly plowed parking spot in front of *Stone Cold Charity*. Putting on hats and gloves, wrapped in down-filled coats, they got out and walked around the outside of the building, Sharon commenting, "Hard to really see what the foundation looks like with all of this snow still in the alley. Maybe we could get the city to bring over a dozer and clean it up a bit, eh, Ahmed?"

"There again, Sharon. Your contacts may be invaluable."

She smiled and led him into the building, nodding to Victoria Blessing, the director of the entire enterprise and a woman whose energy, smile and commitment made *Stone Cold* a haven for the homeless and needy.

"Hi Victoria," Sharon greeted her with a soft wave and the gentle comfort that goes with an established relationship. "I'm not sure that you have met Ahmed Hassan. He is the spiritual leader of the Sikh community and they are looking about Woodland Park for a site to build a temple. Heard that you might be wanting to sell this building and transfer to another location near the business community. Any truth to that?"

"Ya, Ya," Victoria answered with that brilliant smile that she brought to every enterprise. "We really can't serve the homeless way out here...and many of those who need off-priced clothing and household goods find us too far away from their houses. We're looking for property. When we find it, we're gonna want to sell this site. Is it what you're looking for?"

"Well, maybe," Sharon answered, "but winter is a heck of a time to look at structures...and this storm has really locked things up, eh?"

"It has...but I could give the city a call and see if they could send a 'dozer around in an hour and clean the back alley. I can show you around the inside while were waiting. Whad'ya think?"

Sharon looked over at Ahmed, his eyes were glancing around the interior even as Victoria spoke, but now they moved back to hers and he nodded his agreement.

"Sounds good Victoria. You give 'em a call and we'll sort through a few things and get a feeling for the place."

Victoria rang. Ahmed and Sharon wandered and in 20 minutes a front-end loader showed up outside the front door.

They directed it to the back of the building and there it began to clear the snow...at first working down the middle of the alley, pushing the near-slush to the end of the lot, then coming back to move the hulking figures of iced-in donations: sofas, comforters, some appliances, chairs, a dining room set, and several bags of clothing all covered by the frozen snow. Victoria commented again how hard it was to sort through goods that people just dropped off after hours.

"This last storm was awful...snow layered for a few days, then a bit of melt, then frozen and then snow again. Terrible pile of ruined goods."

"They're gonna need some trucks to get this stuff hauled away," Sharon commented, "I'll call Devlin and see if he can shake one down off the maintenance tree."

Another half hour and a dump truck quietly showed up and the loader went to work, scraping from one end of the snow-covered moguls to the other. The truck was half-filled with lost debris when the scooper blade edged into a hump that seemed to be frozen deeply in place. The operator pushed the bulge a bit. Not much improvement, and he gave it a bit of a running jolt and broke it loose.

Nothing apparently associated with furniture, it seemed to be a block of ice frozen around something...not clearly visible. Sharon motioned the operator to push it forward a bit more, maybe shake some of the snow off it. He went to work on it again, and this time, it shed a few layers... some ice, some snow, and then some loose clothing... and then something no one wanted to see...the dirty, smeared searing of frozen, human flesh.

"OH MY GOD!" Victoria screamed. "THAT'S A BODY...A DEAD BODY!"

Ahmed saw it too...in reflex, he reached for the small dagger in his turban, took it to hand and prepared for whatever might follow.

Sharon saw him move, reached out to reassure him and blessed herself, praying that they were looking at a natural rather than a violent death.

The loader operator looked sick...shut the engine down, refused to move it another foot. He paused for a few minutes, then climbed to ground and went over to Victoria. "Gonna have to call the cops, maam."

"You bet'cha," Victoria said, "Call 'em right now. We're gonna go in the building and give everyone all the space they need."

"Good call, Victoria," Sharon said, and turning to Ahmed, she said in a flat, commanding tone, "Let's get in there, Ahmed...now!"

He moved without a sound or a comment, carefully replacing his small weapon into his turban.

Three minutes later, Chester Devlin picked up his phone in the station house and got the report. Death in the alley at *Stone Cold Charity.* Not too alarmed, he said to himself. Storm like this...not too unusual for someone to get caught outside...die of exposure...especially around a charitable building. Still...got to get over there and see that everything is handled right...protocol and all.

He lifted his body from the chair, grabbed a coat and gloves and headed out the door. "Death over at *Stone Cold Charity,*" he told Oswald, "Homeless man caught in the storm...doesn't appear to be homicide."

Three days later, the coroner corrected him. A knife wound into the chest pierced the heart. A note praising Allah stuck to the torso. A fringe of cloth distinct from the victim's clothing remained locked in a clenched fist. Abrasions along the side of his cheek. It all told a sad story.

Reading it, Devlin conjured his own mental resolve. Quiet season was over now. Homicide back in play, and as spring began to gently alter the course of the sun, he took it upon himself to try to set things right...Woodland Park deserved no less.

He surprised himself in asking a silent question, "Where is Kirk?" Pain in the ass all right, but he wanted to pick his brain. He asked around. No one had seen him. Well, he would keep a tight lid on the evidence...explosive in its potential indictment of Muslims. Last thing he needed was some vigilante abuse of anyone in his community.

Within the week, word spread that the dead man had not died of natural causes. "Murder" now sprang to gossipy local lips. Plenty of chatter everywhere. The *Gazette* sent a local reporter down to learn more about what might have killed the poor soul, but Devlin's brief comments barely covered the mystery. "Sadly, we are dealing with murder, and we continue to investigate. When we know more, we will report it."

That left locals on edge, but within two weeks, without fresh facts, they cooled as quickly as the victim lying in the morgue.

Spring progressed. Bingo began to attract a wider following. Amidst a series of failed break-ins, a couple of successful robberies left two more businesses cash-poor and Devlin tried to balance his quiet inquiries about murder with his irritation at the lack of security on the occasional graveyard shift. Stability and safety in Woodland Park began to erode. He asked again, "Where was Kirk?"

KIRK RETURNS

B 9

In the wilderness there is knowledge. In scarcity, there is bounty. Alone, one fills the space of self-awareness with self-reliance. Yet, without family one dies. The rules which pervade the village also touch the soul, guide the body, transmit spirit through winter to the release of spring. Once again, he felt cleansed. Within him there were two faces. One for the tribe. One for his soul. Balance.

Gnawing on some smoked meat, Kirk walked out of the crude, wooden shelter that had been his home for nearly a year. Spring approaching. He felt soft air, knew rising temperatures would shatter ice and clear the river. He took in deep breaths, looked again at his world and praised himself for having survived his self-imposed isolation. Was it over?

He stood, chewing, thinking, reviewing all that he had learned through winter. In this frozen world, nature granted life only if one knew how to court it. He hadn't. He began alone, struggled, nearly perished, then found himself adopted by the tribe. Young men showed him where to find food, how to create warm winter shelter, when to hunt and harvest, how to smoke meat and fish, snare rabbits...fold a seal fin...taught him remedies for minor cuts and bruises. They kept him alive.

He thought about their kindness, instruction and protection. Puzzled the ways in which they remained so disciplined. They knew both the serious skills of survival, and the delightful tricks of diversion. More than once, he had reached for a handful of beads in a hand only to retrieve a small rock. How did they do that? They smiled. They taught him.

He managed to avoid living in a snow tunnel, finding enough scrap wood to shelter himself through winter. A wandering moose in late October filled the common smokehouse with meat and plenty of fat to go with it. Ice fishing reminded him of home and the lakes around Woodland Park. He didn't flourish, but he lived.

Through the winter, he became part of a new family. The tribe smoothed the edges of nature...let him survive blizzards, walk safely amidst traps and snares, feed without fear. Not every hunting venture of his succeeded. Nature had rules and to her, individuals were simply pull-pins on the board of life. But live within the tribe, and one survived. Sobering.

As winter passed, he began comparing native judgment to civilized justice. Criminal law back home applied intellect, written codes and thoughtful penalties to modify behavior. Its watchwords were patience, probation, renewal. Yet, for all its presumed behavioral science, it struggled to cleanse society of the criminal.

Too often, retrieving the best parts of human nature became a reverence for words, a worship of procedures and the handwringing nuances of conviction. The guilty, swept off the streets, reappeared within months, duplicating earlier reports of robbery, assault and fraud. Tiresome retreads.

And then there was murder.

Homicide. The irrevocable act of execution. For him there were no nuances to punishing a killer. And he knew how to do it, how to balance those scales of justice. But what was he...an informal officer of the law, a vigilante or simply nature's agent?

In his adopted tribe, murder produced ejection, isolation and a season of death. In his white man's world, exile... be it prison, probation or personal...never solved the problem.

He had looked it up. Survey said 25,000 deaths a year with no arrests, and that didn't include Chicago, a category all to itself. No justice for those victims whatever, not even the pretense of punishment. In his Indian family, killers were promptly exiled into death. Could he do less?

Nature had its ways. Man had his. Sometimes, one borrowed from the other, and Kirk was happy to do so. When a blindfolded Lady Justice failed to convict a murderer, he, Mr. Scales, could correct the error, and he could do it in the name of natural justice...after all, a principled goal justified a powerful cleansing.

He knew that he could catch a fish and gut it. Mike Carrady taught him that lesson a long time ago. But that was a task, a responsibility. What was its justification? Was he wrong in permanently removing a Woodland Park killer evading justice? No, he concluded. If he could strip a salmon as quickly as a grizzly, he could take life from a murderer as naturally as his tribe would evict a miscreant to die. He was nature's alter ego.

He came back to his moment. Focused on the ice beginning to stir, moaning, rising a bit even as the river began its swell. He finished mauling the bit of moose. Looked around...took a deep breath. Spring in sight. Internal conflicts resolved. Time to go back to his first tribe, Woodland Park.

He looked up at the sky, clear and blue today, measured the height of the sun, assessed its arc and looked toward his lodge. He admitted that it would be nice to slide his body into a full water bath, and that would come in a few weeks, but for now, he lived with his own scent mixed with the musk of smoked survival.

Wouldn't be going home to Lydia. Before he went west, she had taken a new position with Empire Trust in New York. No need to replace her. His log home remained empty, ready to shelter him. The community? He'd just show up one day and walk into *Ole's Donut 'Ole*...my God what would that be like...and order up an apple fritter and good hot coffee. Would anyone have missed him?

Two weeks later, having spent five days in Vancouver buying clothes, adjusting to a western diet and bathing in both tub and shower, he zipped his new travel case, checked his passport and called his driver. Enjoyed an hour's travel through the city as he admired the century old homes that now sold for historic cash, feeling the energy and resilience of a city once focused on beaver fur but now living on the commerce of the Pacific.

He liked the feel of Vancouver, but he liked Woodland Park better, and when he caught his flight to the Twin Cities, he felt as though he were passing from a native womb, slithering through a birth canal, still attached to the placenta of his year's retreat. The plane dropped him into the hands of the midwife, the cord snapped, and he found himself nestled into the land of Devlin, donuts and Deity.

No welcoming committee. Quietly, he made his way home, his cabin waiting patiently for him on the edge of the lake. Entering, he smelled the full scent of a year of leaking pine sap, stale air and the pungent assault of furniture shedding content and filtering air. He opened windows. Left the door ajar. Quietly went about unpacking his case, inspecting the shelves and contents he had left to fend for themselves.

Not bad. Nothing to throw out and however bitter winter's cold had been, it didn't break drained pipes. Caulking remained firmly set between logs, and the fireplace welcomed his attention. He spent a day warming his home, checking dressers and drawers. Took a nap and walked into town.

He strolled, soaking up views so familiar, letting memories roll through his mind: *Marge's Fabric Shop, Holstrum's Hardware, Angus' Tools and Rentals.* Stopped a bit to look at the Acres...reviewing its crazy history, admiring again its careful management by owner, Arnie Arneson who insisted on keeping the land free for kids to play without adult supervision. No organized team sports allowed. A beautiful space, and today full of the noise and thumps of soccer.

He walked on, still having seen no one to greet, wondering if Woodland Park would even remember his name. Finally got to Ole's and paused. Smelled the sweets, heard the murmur of small town talk, paused, then walked in.

The bell on the door rang, people glanced over as was their habit and there was a pause...a small gasp from one table toward the back...and then Ole's voice filled the void. "JONAS! JONAS! JONAS! You are BACK! The greeting reverberated through the entire space and quickly found new life in scattered greetings.

"Jonas...at last."

"Kirk, you devil, thought you left for good, eh?"

"What was her name, Jonas?"

"Did ya get lost in a brewery somewhere in Colorado?"

The greetings went on...embarrassing really, as he waved, smiled his best embrace, let the enthusiasm die down, then turned to Ole and ordered.

"Think maybe I'll have an apple fritter, fresh and hot, eh Ole?"

"Ya, ya, Jonas. I'll pull a couple out of the fryer in the next five minutes...you grab a chair...I'll bring coffee and you can begin to catch up on all the excitement in town."

"Excitement?"

"Oh, ya...we been having all kinds of changing times since you been gone. I hope you had a nice vacation, Jonas, cause you're gonna find some work now, I think, ya."

"Well, let me feed my face, Ole, and then I'll go looking for the one person who knows all about quelling excitement... seen Devlin around lately?"

"Ya, ya. He was in here less than an hour ago. Said something about meeting with the coroner and trying to get a better handle on the latest homicide."

"Homicide? Really? In Woodland Park?"

"You bet'cha. Hard to understand, but by golly, it happened...right there in the alley behind the *Cold Stone Charity*...and that ain't all, don'cha know."

"I don't Ole. What else is going on in this quiet little town?"

"Oh robberies...thieves...nighttime terrors...it's just been awful. I keep waiting for whoever it is to hit my place at night. I take my day's deposits personally into the bank... no more night deposit boxes...I don't care how safe they say it is...been a mess, Jonas...and no one seems to be able to stop it."

"Feed me, Ole, and I'll start to nose around."

"Apple fritter, hot on the plate, coming out right now, Jonas...ya, ya, good to have you back!"

Kirk waved thanks, settled into his chair and began to engage his mind in some of the news. He had been gone a year. Had to have been some changes in town...new people...new issues...and now, new crimes. He sorted through the stories...scanty detail. Figured that he knew where to go next...good ol' Detective Lieutenant Chester Devlin. He growled a lot, but he was a man of integrity and good will...and he liked solving crime. He smiled at that thought and turned to his apple fritter.

TRACY METZGER

O 73

The lizard sensed the sunshine. Left the depth. Found his warmth. Admired by few, he slithered about under the leaves and brush. Only then, in the skittering of his day could he be seen clearly. A pattern of movement. A product of stealth. He survived by nibbling away at small crumbs which others ignored. But he survived.

Tracy Metzger walked into *Ole's Donut 'Ole* with a smile on his face and active, narrow eyes. Couldn't be an easier way to contact local folk and get a good feeling for their news. He enjoyed parking his car nearby and sauntering up to the front door, greeting people with an easy, "Good Morning". Public recognition told him that he was blending right into community.

He was working on his breakfast when the door jingled and a new face walked in...rough edges but a smooth, confident interior. The shouts and greetings surrounding his entry told him plenty...man respected, man embraced... but told him nothing about the fellow's role in Woodland Park.

He watched as the banter turned into reports of local crime, robbery and murder, and he felt the sense of confidence that the whole pastry shop seemed to have in this man, Jonas Kirk. A local icon of justice, Kirk, and he was back in town. Metzger listened, sampled the pulse of the eatery and resolved to ask the Bishop about him. As the banter settled, he quietly finished his bacon, eggs, coffee, paid his bill and slipped away. Without a backward glance, he walked over to St. Mark's and asked to see Father Eggert.

"Good morning, Tracy. What brings you around this morning?"

"Ah, good morning, Father. Taking a morning walk. Figured I could stop in and see how you feel things are going with Bingo. Tone light enough, calling enough games? People believe that they're getting a fair shake?"

"Oh, yes, Tracy. They seemed to have embraced it. I think it's turned into more of a social occasion than a gambling session…small talk all evening…robbery and that murder over near the *Stone Soup Charity*. Everyone's working on the latest gossip."

"Great news…yep, I feel the fun going through the crowd. They do like spinning theories and wondering about what's gonna happen next."

Father Eggert laughed a little, "Yes, they do. I got a phone call telling me that Jonas Kirk is back in town and that will stir the pot even more. First thing we know, they'll be betting on how fast he can help the cops solve our crime wave."

"I saw him drop by Ole's this morning…seemed to get quite a reaction from everyone. Where's he been?"

"I'm not sure. He just quietly disappeared about a year ago. He travels quite a lot but usually spends the heart of the winter here. It was unusual for him to be gone...but... now...well, he's back and we all feel good about that."

"Well, nice to see the town welcoming him. Say, do you think I could get an appointment with Bishop Burkey? Would like to touch base with him and be sure he's happy about how things are going."

"Let me make a call," Eggert replied, and picked up his phone. Short conversation and then he asked, "Can you be over there about 11:30? He'll be happy to talk with you then."

"You bet...have the secretary write me in."

"Done." Eggert confirmed the arrangement and rose. "See you tomorrow evening, Tracy. Keep an eye out for Devlin. He said he would be dropping by and I'd like for him to feel comfortable with everything."

"He is? Well, great! I'll keep an eye out for him. See you then, Father."

He walked on back to Ole's, picked up his car and drove to the Bishop's chancery. Parked and let himself into the waiting room, noting that a couple of local women... Sharon Cunningham and Alice Goodwin were chatting in another office.

Bishop Burkey appeared, cleared his throat, "Ahem, well Tracy, what brings you over today...no trouble I hope?"

"Oh, none...can we settle into your office?"

"Of course," and they retreated, though Burkey left the door open a bit, just to let air keep circulating. As they entered the Bishop's office, Alice and Sharon drifted into the receptionist foyer to continue their conversation.

"So, Alice," Sharon asked, "Just to sum it up, you have no objection if the Sikhs want to try and find a new property for their temple?"

"Oh, no...none at all, Sharon. I think it is very Christian to accommodate them...and that Ahmed is certainly a gentleman. I like him."

Even as they spoke, the Bishop's voice interacted with Tracy Metzger's, and as was her nature, Alice kept her best ear on the Bishop's conversation.

"You're sure...don't want to find any surprises over there..."

"No, none in sight...nothing to hold things up."

"He's happy enough with the sales?"

"Yep."

"Any scheduling problems with Ziggy?"

"Nada. He's all in...and now that we have a code...well, it's gonna work well. Plenty of diversions...just scratch and scram. Gives the crew something to do most nights and keeps everyone looking.

"Good. Anything of concern at all?"

"Just a little interested in this Jonas Kirk. You know him... he's back from somewhere and people seem to really like him."

"Just work around Kirk. And don't be too quick to get to know Devlin either...best to keep them both at a distance."

"You see Kirk as any real problem?"

"No. A bit of a pain in the ass, as they say, but I'll keep an eye on him and let you pick your targets. No strife. Everything looks great. You happy?"

"Damn rights...ooops, sorry about that."

They both laughed.

In the adjoining room, Alice's mind flitted back and forth between her conversation with Sharon and the muddled voice of Bishop Burkey. Reminded herself to sort through his vestments, get them cleaned and pressed for Sunday's service. Already had to throw out one of his sash wraps... stained in the center and frayed on the end...he just didn't take care of things properly.

Amusing to hear him talk to Metzger about *strife* or was it about a *knife*? She knew that his crozier carried a pretty sharp blade in its base. She had asked him once about that, and he just mentioned casually that it was important to have some sort of self-defense available when he was so exposed to the public. Nonsense, she thought! Who would want to hurt a Bishop? Such gibberish. Then again, she heard Jonas Kirk's name and that alone was enough for her to keep her ears open.

She commented to Sharon, "You know, everyone in town will be a-twitter about Jonas Kirk being back in town. Didn't you get to know him pretty well a while back? What do you think of him?"

Sharon paused, considered...finally responded. "He knows a lot, sees a lot and hears a lot. He helps solve problems about town. Now that he's back, I hope he gets involved with the latest flurry of robberies and that homeless man."

"Well, I think he should be *in a hurry*...quite enough gossip going on all over town."

"I'm sure. Well, I have an appointment to meet Ahmed over at *Stone Cold Charity*. See you later, Alice...and don't worry, I'll get the candle wax-savers cleaned up before Sunday."

"Wonderful, Sharon...I know you can *handle all the back waivers*. Say hello to Victoria for me."

"Will do."

As the women left, Metzger concluded his visit with Burkey. "Any word on that murder in the alley."

"Nothing...very unusual death of course...and it has generated some tensions...a bit of bad feeling toward the Muslim community...no evidence revealed yet, but even the Sikhs are being looked at with some suspicion. I heard they carry knives around with them...hidden in their turbans."

Metzger grimaced. "Sad. Very tough to have a part of the town infected with that sort of thing, but Bingo night seems to have grown since that murder was discovered. Still occasional talk about finding the killer. Say, any word on who that homeless guy was?"

"No, just a nameless victim. And you're right, Tracy. Nothing like mystery to get people chatting. Hope they continue to puzzle over it. Well, keep up the good work. Keep the crew happy. Everything I hear suggests we have a success on our hands."

"Oh, I think so...sorry to have it focus on a murder, though."

"Well, yes, but it's a topic...zig on robbery, zag on murder. Sometimes, bad things give us great blessings," Burkey smiled and rose, signaling the end of the conversation.

Hear me and note my words, written in bright letters. Feel me and keep my soul whole. Embrace me and let our lives layer and linger.

Sharon Cunningham shook her head in mild amusement as she left Alice Goodwin. The woman was certainly dedicated to the Altar Society. Responsible for providing care and support for Father Eggert, she carried her concern right over to Bishop Burkey. Well, Sharon thought, it was all innocent enough, and in truth, Alice took the Bishop precisely at his word and conveyed his ideas to the women with great enthusiasm.

Of course, she did not always hear what Burkey said, but she usually had the concept in hand and so far, misunderstood details had not caused her much embarrassment. Still, to hear her confuse a directive to "be sure there is plenty of incense in the sacristy," and announce it as *"a need to be sure that nothing insensitive should be said about sacrilege,"* well, that kept Sharon amused.

Her thoughts drifted away from Alice to Ahmed. She wondered about his interest in *Stone Cold Charity* as a site for a temple. Would its foundation support a second story? The recent homicide in its back alley...not good.

She tried to keep her mind focused on the property as she drove to meet him, but that murder kept seeping into her thinking. What in the world was that all about, really? The police were very quiet about it...even Geraldine had heard nothing from Devlin. There were rumors...speculations... but only one thing was for sure, well two things, well three. He didn't have a name and he hadn't died from natural causes. It was not a suicide. May or may not have had a purpose...probably not robbery...maybe a personal argument.

She frowned a bit as she ran these uncertain bits of information through her head. One of the most challenging things about the victim was that it was very, very difficult to tell when he had been killed.

He was under the snow, so he died sometime during the day or maybe the day before the first Bingo night, but he was not found for over a week, a chunk of ice by then, so time of death remained just a guess. Well, she thought with some private satisfaction, there were ways to induce homicide in such a way as to make the window of death nearly impossible to estimate. She had experience with that. She let her mind drift a little...

Enough! She saw Ahmed standing there in front of *Stone Cold Charity.* Let's see what he thinks about the place.

"Hallo, Sharon," he greeted her as she left her car. "A nice day made nicer by spending some time with you," he smiled.

"Ahmed, you're getting pretty good at the flattery game... and I appreciate it," she laughed. "What is it you want to see here? What do you want to find?"

"Ah, Sharon, let me enjoy the twinkle in your eye. I have some serious property purpose, but now I can enjoy my day much more fully."

"You are shameless," she smiled. "Let's go inside and have a look around."

They entered and immediately heard the boisterously friendly greeting of Victoria Blessing. "Hallo you two... don'cha look nice just walking in off the street...not ready to buy some new duds are ya?"

"Victoria," Sharon smiled, "You're not sizing up your customers very well this morning...a little fatigue from late night dancing?"

"Ya, a little, but another cup of coffee and I'll be wide awake. Want some?"

"Not now...just left Altar Society and Ahmed doesn't drink it. You know we just want to gently assess the space, but I do want to ask, why are you looking to sell the building...planning to close down completely?"

"Don'cha know! Can't shut the charity down of course, but we're just not in a very good location. Good connection with the main streets, and we do see quite a bit of traffic, but people aren't inclined to be stopping to shop a charity shop. Naw. We need to be somewhere that people can just walk over...walk in...and walk their goods home."

"Hate to say it this way," Sharon asked, "But is there much traffic with the homeless?"

"Oh, ya, ya. We see a lot of wanderers, but they can go most anywhere in town to find us. It's local folk who need clothing or little furnishings...those are the ones we have a hard time serving. We need to be closer to them, don'cha know."

"Well, this building certainly works well...lots of open space, plenty of racks, large aisle space, nice parking lot...I guess it fits the bill in almost every respect except proximity to its main shoppers, eh?"

"Ya. Now Ahmed, you been pretty darn quiet...what're you thinking...really interested in the place?"

"Interested? Yes Victoria, interested, but not committed. As I look at the space, what I see is opportunity to remodel, but also a need to expand the walls, and to even consider a second story and temple space would require a significant investment. Still, it does have a good feeling about it, and it is a site that I want to bring before my local council."

"Oh, got'cha. The space isn't for everyone...works for us, but we need to find something closer to town...some location where a dead guy doesn't lie under the snow for a week before anyone finds him," she grimaced. "Jeez... anyone find out who he is...any names, Ahmed?"

"Ah, nothing Victoria...that was such a tragedy...terrible loneliness, and death in the cold is a bitter, sad way to leave this earth? And no one even knew his name."

"Gotta buy that one hundred percent. Damn wish I'd been over here all evening, but like everyone else I was sitting in St. Mark's Hall arranging Bingo cards and talking up a storm. Seemed like such a friendly gathering...well, I guess it was...just didn't leave anyone in a position to pull this guy into shelter before someone sent him to another world."

"Very sad indeed, Victoria. Well, thanks for letting us take a look around. I'll be consulting with my adviser, Sharon here," Ahmed smiled, "and see if the Sikh community might want to examine the opportunity further."

As they walked out, they threw a wave to Victoria and nonchalantly locked arms, laughing about something that surfaced between them.

Don't know if they know it, Victoria said to herself, But I think they're looking at more than property...ya, for sure.

GOSSIP

I 30

Scheduled uncertainty. Erratic stability. Strategies.

"Welcome back...welcome back," Father Eggert greeted faces known and new as they entered St. Mark's Hall. More than a month now since Tracy Metzger called out that first Bingo ball and the crowd continued to grow. Bishop Burkey had been right...give people some time together, a little luck and a lot of laughter and chatter. They'll be back. Now, here he was, at the front door, instead of backstage working to get things going. Profits grew. Clearing an easy $3,000 a week and Metzger was every bit as good as the priests in Iowa said he would be. If this keeps up, they'll be able to raise the cost of the cards...supply and demand, he smiled.

"Good evening, Sharon. Good to see you. And Geraldine, know anything about Lt. Devlin? Will he be joining us?"

"Not tonight, Father. He's got some commitments down at the precinct that's gonna keep him busy...but he might be here next week."

Sharon looked over at her as they entered the hall. "When does he decide whether to come on over, Deeni...just on impulse? Or is it that no-cop-on-the-street stuff again."

"Yeah, that's it. Never really knows 'til the last minute... and I gotta say he's getting pretty damned tired of it. Chasing down suspects for attempted break-ins, and then the occasional robbery, is wearing thin, and that homicide, hell, he won't even say anything to me 'bout what he knows...and he knows something, that's for damn sure."

"Well," Sharon smiled, "I'm sure that you could wrap your legs around that problem if you want to."

"Well, miss Lady India, aren't you tip-toeing in the gutter a little, eh?"

"Oh, a ripple," Sharon smiled, "but I think that you may know more than you think you know."

"Well, my close, confidential, reliable, intimate friend, let me tell you something that I do know."

Sharon stopped, "What?"

"I know that the way that you look at that brown skinned, bearded statue in a turban sends out a radio signal a block away. What's with you and that Muslim guy anyway?"

"Deeni...whatever you think you are seeing...it's simply imagination. Ahmed and I have had some conversation about the Sikhs...and they are not Muslim by the way... about the Sikhs buying some property on which to build a temple. He asked for some advice, and I enjoy sharing ideas with him."

"And just what idea do you have in mind?"

"Not that one...well, not yet, she smiled. "Right now, he's just looking for some property that has a few acres of land. *Stone Cold Charity* has that, but it's pretty far out of town. I think he needs something a bit closer."

"Hmmm, well I may know something about that...I hear a lot you know...part of my daily business...getting to find out what's going on."

"Oh, yes," Sharon smiled, "You're a treasure in the information department, Deeni. But are you kidding... about having some idea about property?"

"No, not kidding," Deeni smiled, "You should wander over to see Fred Daggert when he and Gordo come by to check on food supplies and stuff... during the intermission. I think he has some land on his hands. You might find something that you can lay before Ahmed.

"Let's just stick to the land business, Deeni, not the bed business."

Deeni laughed, "Stay focused, eh? On what, Sharon? Time to go to confession yet? You still do don't you?"

"Don't we all," Sharon smiled, then arranged her cards, waiting for Tracy Metzger to call out the first ball.

He appeared within minutes, rolled the cage and hollered out the first number of the evening: I-18...and on it went. Ninety minutes later, he called intermission, and Fred Daggert's crews opened the doors to the serving areas. Lines formed then disappeared. Silence and salt passed from table to table. When the pressure eased, Sharon went over to Daggert.

"Hi Sharon. Really nice to see you out here enjoying yourself...Bingo seems to have captured the crowd, eh?"

"It has, Fred. Say, Geraldine Wright was telling me that you might have some property that could be of interest to the Sikhs...you know Ahmed Hassan asked me to look around for something...we even spent some time over at *Stone Cold Charity* looking it over."

"Whaddya think of it, Sharon?"

"Oh, it has some good interior space...open...could certainly remodel easily enough, but it's a bit away from the Sikh community and it would probably be a lot cheaper for them to build something from scratch than raise a second story."

"Yeah. I heard that the charity needed to relocate...get a little closer to town...guess they and the Sikhs are looking in the same area, eh?"

"Well, not the same neighborhood I don't think, but they don't see that structure as something that they can build into their future. You have any ideas?"

"I really can't explore it with you right now, Sharon, but drop by main *ZigZag* tomorrow...say about 2:00 pm and we can talk. I might have some helpful suggestions."

"Sounds good, Fred...now let me have one of those burgers you keep cooking...how do you keep it all tasting so fresh...delicious really."

"Trade secrets, Sharon," Fred laughed. "But I share free samples...come by tomorrow...I'll give you some."

"Will see you then...about two."

She walked back to her cards, passing Tracy Metzger who stopped her long enough to ask, "Sharon, been looking around for Lt. Devlin. Seen him anywhere tonight?"

"No, Tracy...I'm pretty sure he is on assignment...not gonna make it tonight, but Deeni says he may be here next week."

"Well, good to know. I'll tell Daggett that he'll need to bring in a little extra food," he laughed. Guess I'll get back and get the balls rolling again," he laughed. "Got to keep the money flowing."

Sharon smiled a gentle goodbye, returned to her seat wishing that she knew why she found Tracy so unappealing. She likened him to a cheap mouthwash. From a distance, fresh. Up close, sour.

Oh, my gosh, she said to herself, what am I doing...turning into some kind of a detective? I just don't like the guy... leave it at that...but she couldn't. What in the world drove a man in good health to concentrate on managing and promoting Bingo? Money? Yes, but how much...maybe, she asked herself, she should ask from what source... certainly not the evening cards themselves. And if his payment was coming from the parish, how was it able to keep him suitably engaged and still raise money to help the various causes...even help run the administration. And what did he do from Thursday to Wednesday?

Enough, Sharon, she brought herself up short. Have a good time tonight, think about Metzger tomorrow. Have some fun.

"Hey, Miss Smooth Hips!" Geraldine shouted, "Get them over here and sit. He's gonna' make some calls. I can't cover all your cards and mine too...and I wanna' win."

Sharon Cunningham sat, gracefully, arranged her cards and let her mind focus on Fred Daggert...really a nice member of the community. Wonder why he doesn't expand into another location...there's room...well, may not be the best of financial times, but maybe he'll find a way.

She felt the presence of Ahmed. Glanced over to the wall where he was talking with Robert Olson. As though on command, he turned and looked at her, smiled. She fanned her face with her hand, then smiled right back and let her thoughts go free. Oh my! What a fine figure of a man... haven't used that word for a while...too long...*a man*.

CONNECTION

G 49

Rejoinders renewed.

The phone again. Devlin picked it up, "Woodland Park Police...is this an emergency?"

"If there were an emergency, why would I be calling you?"

"What the...gimme your name, right now!"

"Can you write?"

"I can assure you, I will remember...your name?!"

"How about Jonas Kirk."

Silence...three seconds passed. Then, more quietly, "Kirk? Kirk? That's really you?"

"So, what was it that Arnold said, 'I'm baaaack'."

"You little pissant...you take some kind of powder for a year and now just show up...for no reason? Are you coming home or just moving through our little town on your way to somewhere...to nowhere?"

Softly, "I'm back to stay, Devlin. Been in town a few days. Took time out from life for a while…finally figured I'd like to rejoin it and that even included you."

"Not sure that's a good thing, Kirk, but your timing's perfect."

"How so?"

"Well, if you had shown up a month ago, I would'a asked what you knew about a loser dying out behind the *Stone Cold Charity*…but you weren't here, so maybe you can help me a little."

"That sounds like you have questions you can't answer, Devlin. Not much has changed since I left, eh?"

"What has changed, Kirk, is that we have new people coming into town…we have a little religious tension…we have that pain-in-the-ass Bishop Burkey floating some damn Bingo game to milk more money out of people."

"That's it?"

"And we have the city budget blown to crap…no money, sometimes no nighttime security…multiple attempted break-ins and a couple of serious robberies. Stress all around."

"Well, is *Ole's Donut 'Ole* still open?"

"Damn right!"

"Well, then I think the fundamentals are in place. Still, you sound upset. Spending enough quality time with Geraldine?"

"What the hell are you talking about?"

"Now, now, Devlin. You are a fairly good cop, but you're out of the loop if you don't know that your trips down to Winona have been recorded, catalogued and stored in the memory of every gossip who shows up at Ole's."

"They don't know shit."

"But they guess, Devlin...and they talk. No matter. So, you are settled in your personal life...is that a nicer way to ask?"

"It is. I am. Are you?"

"Today...yes. Now how about we go somewhere out of the way, maybe over to the *Splintered Pine*...have some coffee, a bite to eat and we can talk. Would be nice to see your face...if you can keep food off it."

"Twenty minutes."

"Done."

Don't care how long it takes, Kirk thought, I'm gonna get there after him...let him squirm just a little...then see if he has something interesting to say.

He parked a half block away, keeping an eye on the entry, checking his watch, finally releasing a breath as Devlin's old Ford Fairlane pulled up in front of the coffee joint. Now, we'll see.

He waited another five minutes, walked in and found him at a table in the back, nose buried in the menu, a perky brunet waitress with pad in hand politely waiting for the order she was trying to pull from him.

"So, something more than the stack and bacon."

"Damn right. Uhhmmmm, o.k. Let's go with a side of hash browns, another side of ham and some stuffed sausages to go right on with the cakes...then another coffee and keep an eye on me. I don't like to run out."

"Gee, Mr. Policeman, you don't have to worry about me... I'm the one that needs to worry about you, right," and she smiled that genuine smile that told Devlin that he had found the right kind of service.

"Right you are...oh, here comes another customer...the late, great, now returned, Jonas Kirk. Ready to order, stranger?"

"I'll have a mushroom omelet, three eggs, coffee and a biscuit. How's that for comfort food, eh Devlin?"

"You don't need to please me, Kirk. Just be sure she heard you."

"I heard you, dearie. Loud and clear. Be back soon."

She turned and left even as Kirk quietly sat. He looked at Devlin, assessed the state of his clothing, unmarked by spilled food and relatively fresh for this time of the day.

"You learnin' how to press and dress, Devlin?"

"I learn what I have to learn...and right now, my knowledge is a little scanty about a recent murder...first one since you left, and that gives me something to think about, Kirk."

"You mentioned something about robberies too...what's with that?"

"Wish I knew. We are practically having a crime wave... ever since that Bingo crap opened up at St. Mark's the town's been goin' to hell...not the purpose of the Church I didn't think..."

Kirk paused, let "dearie" pour his coffee, sampled her morning scent which was pleasant enough, and waited for her to move on back to the kitchen.

Devlin watched as she disappeared. "So, Kirk, where in the hell have you been?"

"Well, away. Far away," he smiled. "Spent the last year with a native Indian tribe up in Alaska, avoiding grizzly bears, cooking my own food and patching up a small pile of clothing to get me through the winter. The cabin was old, creaky, sometimes leaky and flexible enough not to be blown over in a storm. I learned a lot...about myself, about nature, about the ways of native justice and when I felt myself in balance, I came back to Woodland Park."

"Is that a good thing?" Devlin responded.

"I could have gone anywhere, but to tell the truth...and it may be the only one I tell you...I like it here. But I don't like a town full of crime, especially murder. So, empty your mouth and let me hear the story. I'm interested. I won't interrupt 'til you're done...least I'll try not."

"Sounds to me like you just took a powder...but I'll hear more about that later. Here's what's happened the last month or so. First, St. Mark's decided to start a weekly Bingo game to raise some money. The city should have had the same idea and maybe I could get a raise. Anyway, not long after they started calling out Bingo numbers, we began experiencing a series of attempted break-ins and a couple of serious robberies. No one arrested. Can't find them."

"Anyone stealing the night's haul of Bingo money?"

"No."

"Stealing any time in particular?"

"Well, not really. All the successful robberies have been on a Bingo night, but there's nothing to read into that."

"Successful ones? There have been more?"

"Oh, yes. Two, three times a week. Hell, I get morning reports and there's the list...almost every day... from various merchants...that someone tried to break in...just didn't succeed. One night we caught a guy trying to get into *ZigZag.* Turned out all he wanted was something to eat but he had nothing to do with the other jobs. Common enough to see back entry attempts to some of the bars. Still...some of these attempts are almost amateurish."

"A pattern?

"Not sure. We're lightly staffed on all of the graveyard shifts, some nights there are no patrols at all between midnight and 6:00 am."

"So, the pattern seems to be that you don't catch anyone. Is that it?

"Well, yeah, but hell, just might be too many sleepy patrolman...or too few of them...I don't know for sure. Been close to catching burglars a couple of times. Gonna re-schedule staff. See what happens. Might just be coincidences.

"I don't like coincidence, Devlin...it's usually a veil in front of an answer."

"I'll keep that in mind...I'm a hell of a lot more concerned about the murder."

"Why?"

"Cause there are signs that it may have been the work of some kind of Muslim terrorist."

"What? Here in Woodland Park? Come on now..."

"I know. I know. But I'm gonna tell you something privileged, Kirk...not a word of this to leak out..."

"I'm listening."

"Public doesn't know this, but when the Coroner started going through the dead guy, he found three things that we keep quiet. One, the guy was killed with a knife... sharp, long, lethal."

"Curious...kill a homeless man. Why? Certainly not robbery."

"Not likely. The other two things are more worrisome. We found a note frozen to his chest between his clothes. In Arabic...said something like "God is Great".

"Oh. That's more serious...Muslim terrorism? In Woodland Park?

"There's more, a bit of cloth, bright red, locked in one hand of the victim...as though he reached out in defense when he saw the knife...we think we're gonna connect it with some of those Sikhs...those turban things they wear. Heard from someone that they carry knives up in those wraps too, even combs. Wouldn't surprise me if we were to find a needle and thread if we unwound the right turban. Hell, I don't know."

"I don't really remember there being many Muslims or Sikhs in the city before I left, Devlin...they come in as a group or what...in just a year?"

"A small group of Muslim families moved down from St. Cloud about six months ago. But the Sikhs have been edging into the city over the past couple of years. Nice enough people. Quiet. Looking to become part of the community I guess. I don't know so much about the Muslims. They stay pretty much to themselves."

Kirk paused in his thinking to take a quick look at Devlin's chest. One small bite of pancake stuck on his shirt, just above his belt, but syrup drops near middle of his belly provided the glue to hold a couple of pieces of sausage right in place. Might be a cache for a late day snack.

Kirk motioned to Devlin's shirt with a closed hand. "What all you carryin' there, the beginning of supper?"

Devlin didn't even look. Just took his napkin and wiped the general area. "Satisfied?" He stared at Kirk.

"No. Here try this," and he held out his hand with a small piece of wood. Devlin looked, curious and reached for it. Kirk closed his hand, moved it slightly and opened it again. Now Devlin saw a quarter.

"What the hell are you doing, Kirk?"

"Just trying to remind you that things are not as they seem. Need to look behind the public view, Lieutenant. Muslims and Sikhs may catch the eye, but murder can come from any direction. Slight-of-hand works in many settings, even murder."

"You learn that in a poker game, Kirk?"

"No, I learned it last winter, surviving in Alaska."

"I'm impressed, but not convinced," Devlin snorted, "Muslim's seem frustrated...smoldering...could lead to murder."

Kirk shifted back into full listening mode.

"So, what exactly is it that I might do to help, Devlin. I am at your service...I will even pay for this meal just to ease your pain."

"Too nice, smart ass, but I'll take it. Christ, the city is so poor my paycheck is barebones...no raise at all. Well, I don't have any suspects for anything, Kirk. Seems to me that the whole robbery thing must have something to do with Bingo distractions, but what I don't know. Now, the murder in the alley...well, if that was designed to set off some anti-Muslim sentiment, we could have a bad situation. I've been sitting on that info for over a month, but how much longer...don't know. Got any thoughts?"

I didn't have a full set of ideas, but I had the beginnings of some, and my experience with Devlin was that I was far better off sorting through things awhile before tying him up with an action agenda.

"You've given me some things to think about, Devlin. I'm just back. Let me keep making the rounds and reintroducing myself to a few people. Give me a couple of weeks and I'll see what I can find."

"That's about as long as I can wait, Kirk. The *Gazette* is all over me about details. If I gotta give them some, it won't be pretty."

"Just keep stalling them. Other news will take up the front page."

"Well, that might be, but it would have to be bad news."

"Couple of weeks, Devlin."

"O.K.," he slurped the last of his coffee, wiped his mouth but not his chest, and rose to go. "I'm gonna be at the Bingo hall tonight...you wanna drop by. I'll introduce you to a couple of people."

My, I thought, Devlin was getting nicer...introducing me to new faces. Well, I did need to get to know a few of them. Others, I just needed to get back into a conversation. Good place to start.

"You bet. I'll see you there...may buy some cards and win a few bucks."

"That would not make you popular, Kirk. Buy six of them and moan about your losses...that would be better."

Devlin slipped out of his chair and headed for the door. "Leave a good tip. I'll see you tonight."

And he was gone. I sat there for another half hour, sipping coffee, thinking my thoughts, practicing some of the introspective review of life and people that I had learned the past year. I had an idea about the robberies, but the murder sounded like a genuine problem...a death to create chaos in my tidy hometown. Didn't like it. Needed to solve it.

ANXIETY

N 36

Only the night gives us truths, reveals our most feared reality. Dream away...and away...and away.

Bishop Leland Burkey rolled over in his bed, moaned softly, arranged blankets to suit the temperature and slipped back into sleep. The dream resumed. A peaceful setting...nurturing, complete. Upright on an inflated raft, he paddled himself easily across the lake, birds chittering, light reflecting with shimmering effect. It was morning, the sun still not quite above the tree line. Exercise...a delightful part of his days. The crossing nearly complete, he shaded his eyes to catch the edge of the dock, reached out as he drifted toward it, so close...and missed. Missed!

Fear flooded his arms and chest! Simple strokes no longer worked, and progress became panic. The current, suddenly stronger, swept him away from the wooden landing and into the larger body of water, now a river. White foam funneled into narrows where rocks seemed to block every path. He paddled furiously to find safe passage, angry that his crossing had failed, fearful that his fate would be sealed by unseen currents. Swirling water sloshed from the river into his raft. Out of control!

A deep dig with the paddle to right the course left him empty-handed. Exhausted, he retched as water filled his face. He looked to the skies for an escape, found none. Then, the edge, and he was tumbling through the mists of the falls. Flailing! Flailing! He screamed!

His voice awoke him and even as he clasped the edge of the mattress he felt the sweat of his terror squish on the inside of his pajamas. He stayed motionless, listened for he knew not what, and finally opened his eyes. Tasting bile, he wiped his mouth with his pillow case. The terror lingered briefly, receded as he regained a full sense of where he was...in bed...what time it was...5:00 a.m. Slowly, he took control of his present moment, arose and walked to the kitchen. He turned on the table light, sat and let his still labored breathing gradually subside.

Rational thinking at last. Why in heaven's name would he have such a dream? His sleep was usually flawless, as befits a bishop. But here, tonight, he found himself panicked by a sense of failure, and he began to sweat a little more as he acknowledged his fear. His plan was failing.

It was a simple gambit. Create community hysteria about a Muslim threat. Persuade every parishioner that a Holy War had been unleashed by radical immigrants. Then reassure the public even as he highlighted the danger. Rouse his Catholic following as he spoke about safety, havens and religious protection. His voice would fill a void in Woodland Park, perhaps the Twin Cities, and overnight, Bishop Leland Burkey would become synonymous with a Christian, Catholic defense of the faith.

Elevation, recognition, influence, churchly power... earthly rewards...those were the words that caught his attention, defined his future. Three years ago, Father Lockhart's work in India had nearly managed it for him, but his sudden death left Burkey grasping for a new path to the Curia. He had to scramble ruthlessly to keep Sharon Cunningham from becoming the icon of Lockhart's death, from being seen as a modest, but deeply wounded survivor of an extraordinary mission.

Using slippery words about "ill-advised forms of religious intimacy" and subtle references to the "seductive dangers of a long-distance missionary assignment", he forced her into the background of every review of Lockhart's career...but burying her status did nothing to elevate his.

Now, a new opportunity, a diocesan fight against terrorism. It could revive his reputation, focus attention on his message...and on him. Might elevate him to Archbishop... would certainly give him a public platform and access to conservative members of the Vatican.

Yet, here he was, more than a month after the discovery of that frozen corpse, still stuffed with frustration, kept impotent by the coroner's silence. He could do nothing about warning the Catholic community until the police revealed their findings, and he needed that to happen soon...very soon. Surely, they had found the obvious clues left aboard the dead man. Muslim terrorism had come to Woodland Park, but he couldn't sound the alarm unless there were some findings of evidence ...by the coroner... by the police...by someone in official rank.

Today's news. Anything there? He turned on the radio, settled in with "*Roxie and Mike*" and some early morning coffee.

"*...and so I said to both of them, 'You empty the garbage and do it right, and I'll keep filling it up for you. Let you keep your jobs'...yep, that's what I said, Rox.*"

"*Mike, you have such a gentle way about you, especially when it comes to city services. Ever think that one of those gentle fellows is gonna put your ass in the can before he tosses it into the back of the truck.*"

"*Not a chance, Rox. I just looked at my waistline and realized that I'm too heavy to lift.*"

"*I am not amused, Mike. Do something to brighten my day...tell me some news.*"

"*Dot...dot...dot...calling everyone in the Twin Cities... check your garbage bins and alleys...be sure there are no bodies there, no broken chairs, no piles of carpet, but especially no bodies.*"

"*Really, Mike...that's all you got...dead men in the alleys... oh, wait, I remember...police actually found one about a month ago... right here in Woodland Park, right?*"

"*Yep...remember his name, Rox?*"

"*No...don't think I ever heard one. But murder! Whoa! They find out who did it?*"

"*Not a sound from City Hall, nor the police.*"

"*Well, they probably know a lot more than their telling, Mikie boy...my money is on that cute detective, Chester something...what's his name?*"

"Chester Devlin, Rox. Come on...you know you have a crush on him...and he solves crimes around here. Bet he has some answers that he's keeping to himself."

"Yah, yah. Gotta be. Well, Mikie, after the session today, why don't you Big Boy Up and go interview him...see what he knows."

"After the show today, Rox, I'm gonna find a quiet place to sleep and let the world clean up its own problems... and it will do it better with "Scrubs" the most durable cleaning brush on the market."

"Oh, Mike...there you go again...commercials. I'm gonna spend the rest of my day playing some music like, "Smoke Gets In Your Eyes" and it fills a party room too."

"Got a better one, Rox. Try "Whose Gonna Drive You Home,"...'cause I might not.

"You have to, Mikie, it's in my contract. Fine print...you gotta learn to read."

"We'll see Miss Roxie...well, let's send it back to Morning Notes with Rolf and Ray."

"Need my whole name, dude: Roxie Rochambeau. It's in my contract. (laughing). I'm outta here, complaining again, boo on you, Mikie."

None of this chatter was what Burkey wanted to hear, but they were right about one thing. If he wanted to know what was going on, he should just go see Devlin himself. Demand some answers on behalf of a concerned public. He dressed, ate a light breakfast of toast, yogurt and blueberries. Hated to ask Devlin for anything, but maybe he'd release some information if they sat face-to-face.

"Got a call on line one, Lieutenant."

"Oh, damn, what now?" Devlin muttered. He picked up his phone, pushed a button and greeted the caller, "Mornin', Devlin here."

"Ah, yes...the detective...how nice to hear your voice," Burkey began, then paused. "I was wondering, Lieutenant Devlin if you might like to drop by the Chancery this morning, perhaps at 11:00. I would appreciate a bit of an update on the murder of that poor, homeless soul a month ago...you know, behind *Stone Cold Charity*."

"I would not."

Long pause, then the Bishop resumed. "Oh, would some other time today work into your schedule a little better?"

"It would not."

"So, you are not available to speak about that tragedy at all?"

"I am...but you will have to come here. I don't make house calls."

"Well," Burkey sniffed, "Of course...your schedule, demands, high crime reports lately and all...of course, I understand. Could you see me sometime late morning?"

"Be here at 11:00 a.m. We can talk."

"So glad to hear you can accommodate me, Lieutenant. I'll be there."

Devlin placed the phone back on his pedestal. Burped.

He sat back in his chair and let his mind begin to wander. Burkey was so pompous...a demanding, inquisitive, highly curious prelate who wanted to push back on an information blackout surrounding a murder...more than a month-old murder. Why? A pain in the ass. No one in the press had been speculating about it. So why does the Bishop have a sudden interest? Well, so long as the Coroner didn't feel the need to speak about his findings, the Bishop could sit with him, but he wasn't gonna learn anything, nada.

Promptly at 10:55, Burkey arrived and Oswald directed him to Devlin's office. They sat across from one another, the Bishop in a hard, wooden chair with protruding vertical ribs to hold his back upright...a devil's plaything he thought...so uncomfortable.

Devlin rested in a heavily padded, spring supported, leather chair in which he rocked at a tempo set by his mood. Right now, it moved slowly, constantly, and he looked at the air above the Bishop's head, wondering who would start this conversation. He would.

"So, Your Honor, what brings you down here this morning...you mentioned something about the death of the homeless man a while back."

"Indeed, Lieutenant Devlin, as you know, I am the spiritual shepherd of a considerable flock of saints and sinners here in Woodland Park and elsewhere in the larger metro area. The reported death of a poor, vagrant behind the *Stone Cold Charity* gave some alarm to my people, and I wanted to know what I can say to reassure them."

"Tell 'em we ain't found the killer."

"Oh, my...well of course not, I suppose...else we would have heard about it on the news. But might there be other information you could share. Cause of death perhaps... any information about tattoos, scars, clothing that would identify the victim...clues to who might have been responsible...that sort of thing?"

"No."

"Some have said that it might be a random killing for a religious purpose to inflame local feelings. Could you say...was the victim Muslim?"

"No."

"No, he was not a Muslim or no you could not say?"

"No."

Hmmmm. Bishop Burkey paused, considered where he might go next. Unlikely that he would be going very far.

"Please, Lt. Devlin, is there anything that you can say that I can bring to the St. Mark's Parish and the diocese in general?"

"I can say that we are continuing our investigation and when it is concluded, I will have a statement."

Silence. Burkey considered how long he wanted to continue with this. Keep asking and Devlin might become a little suspicious. So far no one was looking at him.

And then.

"I do have one question for you, Your Excellency."

"Yes, how can I be of service?"

"Victoria Blessing said you were hanging around *Stone Cold Charity* along about closing time...you know, the day we think the guy was killed...doing some shopping, walking the store...casing the joint, as they say. That true?"

Ooooh! That caught him by surprise. He paused to digest the question, sat up a bit, elevated his chin and gave Devlin just the story he thought would satisfy him. The truth, but not the whole truth.

"Oh, yes, Alice and I delivered some clothing for the Charity and looked at some of Victoria's inventory. About to leave and then used the restroom," Burkey began. Paused as though collecting his thoughts. Looked into Devlin's eyes.

"Apart from that, it was merely a stopping place on our way over to the Bingo hall where I was to consecrate the project...gave it my blessing and apparently to good result. It is making a lot of money for the parish, you know." Burkey dropped his voice in descending tone for the last sentence. Confident, relaxed, assertive...not to be questioned.

Devlin looked at the Bishop very closely as he gave his answer. Color normal, eyes meeting his comfortably, occasional pause in his flow of words...no panic...all just right. Well, giving Burkey a little word challenge was a good thing. Kept him on his heels. Kept him in his place. He was a tiresome man.

"Glad to hear it. Wish City Council could figure out a way to raise some money...well, that should be it for now, Bishop. Keep watching the news for any further updates.

Say, you might spend a little time with *Roxie and Mike* in the morning. Even if they don't know anything, they'll entertain you...that's for sure." You have a good day now, your Highness...is that a term Catholics use, eh?"

"It is <u>not</u>."

"Well, maybe they should. I like the way it sounds," Devlin smiled, then went on, "Take care. Be sure to listen carefully in confessions...someone might say something that could help us."

Burkey had been through that confessional sanctity issue with Devlin before, and he wasn't going to waste any more time with him.

"Good day, Lieutenant. Keep up the good work. The community follows you very closely. Everyone wants to hear who killed that poor homeless man. Do we even know his name?"

"We don't. We may not ever, but I do plan to find out who killed him."

Burkey slowly turned away. "As indeed you must, Lieutenant...as indeed you must."

VOICES

O 71

Sampling community. Sharing news.

Seemed like old times. Entering St. Mark's Hall reminded Kirk of his youth...his years in grammar school...the events and socials they had here...and now he was walking into it once again...for Bingo.

How times have changed, he smiled.

Opened the door and began running into people he had missed. Geraldine Wright identified him for the world, "Geezus, my God, it's Jonas Kirk! Where the hell have you been, Kirk?"

He felt the stares from people around her and knew any answer would be incomplete so far as Geraldine was concerned. He tried. "Been up north looking for a challenge, Geraldine...you know, more snow and ice."

"How far up north?"

"Southern Alaska."

"Oh my God...what's up there besides bears, seals and Eskimos?"

"Lessons, Geraldine."

"You back knowin' more than before?"

"I hope."

"Oh, sure, I understand that...seen Devlin yet?"

"I have."

"He fill you in about what's been goin' on around here?"

"He did."

"You gonna get involved?"

"I am."

"Got more than two words for me, Kirk?"

"Yes, I do."

"You are a bit of an asshole, Kirk...you know that don'cha?"

"I do."

"Get on with you. See who can remember you...circulate, Mr. Clean."

"I will."

He moved away with a smile, noting to himself how much he always enjoyed seeing Geraldine and thankful again that she survived the attempt to poison her back in the day...when the Rubber Ducky Car Wash was robbing and threatening people. Well, days past.

He noticed Sharon Cunningham visiting with a tall, brown, handsome man who wrapped his head in a dark green turban. They seem to be conversing in a kind of shorthand... probably had spent some time together...a nice thought for Sharon who, so far as he knew, had been completely unattached since her return from India. Hmmm. Wonder if that is where she met this fellow.

He moseyed over, tossing an eye of recognition, a nod of appreciation to some faces he recognized. Sidled up alongside Sharon, caught her attention and threw a glance at her companion. She noted it.

"Hi Jonas. So good to see you back home again. Sometime soon, we should have a bite of lunch and you can tell me where you've been...and why."

"Hello Sharon. You bet...we can do that. Nice to be back that's for sure. New faces I haven't met," and he glanced at her conversationalist.

"Oh, Jonas, pardon me...this is Ahmed Hassan, leader of the local Sikh community and a good friend looking for property to site a temple. Ahmed, this is Jonas Kirk, a local icon who seems to solve murders so nicely that sometimes you'd think he was at the scene."

"How do you do, Ahmed. Sharon is always very kind introducing me...she has experience with the world of mischief having spent a good deal of time in India, as I'm sure she has reported."

"So good to meet you, Jonas! I have heard many good things about you from many people other than Sharon, although she is one of my very best sources of information. Of her misbehavior, I have very little experience, but there is always the future," he smiled.

Kirk cast a nod over his shoulder. "Geraldine told me you were looking for a place to build a new temple here in Woodland Park. How's that going?"

"Slowly, but we are making progress. I think we will be having promising conversations with some local businessmen, but for now it is still a search."

"Well, I'll keep my ears open. People like to tell me secrets...bring me up to date, I guess. If I hear anything, I'll pass it on."

"Thank you, Jonas. We value nothing more than being able to fit in and contribute to our local community. Woodland Park is a bit of a new name for us, but we feel comfortable with its character and its boundaries...all very promising."

Kirk nodded goodbye, lifted an inquiring eye toward Sharon, and moved on, drawn by the appearance of Father Eggert on the stage. He moved up alongside the platform, said hello, asked if he could get an introduction to Tracy Metzger.

"Oh, sure, Jonas. He should be along here most anytime. Say, have you had a chance to meet Fred Daggert, one of the owners of *ZigZag*? They provide the catered food here each Wednesday."

"Not yet...is he around?"

"A little later I think, near intermission time."

"I'll look forward."

"Wonderful...oh, we're pretty close to start time."

"Guess I'll get some cards and find a seat, Father. Looks like a great crowd...financial success?"

"Surprisingly...yes. See you a bit later."

"I'll look for you when I get a bite of *ZigZag*."

He wandered about. Looked up and saw Devlin waving, his hand no higher than his shirt pocket. But he caught the motion, moved over next to him and sat down.

"Gonna play, Devlin?"

"Not tonight. But I like for the crowd see me...police presence makes 'em feel comfortable...safe."

"Well, I'll play four cards...$20 is a fair price I guess."

"Once again, Kirk...for a guy with no job you seem to always have money...I'm sure you can cover four cards before they raise the price. Crowds have been surprisingly large."

"Really?"

"Yep...oh, here's Tracy."

Out from behind the curtain, Tracy Metzger greeted the crowd with a big, "HALLO WOODLAND PARK...LET'S WIN SOME MONEY!"

The world of Bingo got underway. Kirk heard the calls, marked his cards, found nothing unsettling, relaxed. For the next hour, the balls rolled out, Metzger called the numbers, mixed in a few jokes and gave plenty of attention to the winners.

Finally, Metzger called out The Evening Special. "Gonna go back to that old favorite," he said. 'Ten and Out'. You Know the score. I call ten balls, and if there is a Bingo in that array, the prize is $500."

The ooohs and aaahs came echoing back to him, and he smiled, glanced at the full house and began the call.

Kirk paid close attention to the balls being drawn.

N 33; I 18; O 72 and they continued. Could see nothing of any sort of manipulation...kept one eye on his card, marking down the numbers...getting closer to the winning Bingo call. He began to get excited. He did like to win.

G 48...He had that...just one number away now...he felt excitement rising inside.

B-53. "Whoops," Metzger corrected himself. "Should be G-53, folks." Kirk waited for the last call.

N 36 ...Damn, nothing there on his card. Damn.

The groans and loud protests came from all sides of the hall. Lots of people close, but no winners. Kirk reminded himself that the odds had to favor the house. Wondered what the chances were to win in a 10 draw Bingo game. Something to find out.

As he switched his thoughts to a talk with the *ZigZag* guy, something ran across the back of his mind...the way Metzger called those numbers. Something...he really disliked losing...even at Bingo.

The crowd rose to enjoy sandwiches and drinks and he got up.

"Devlin. Take me over and introduce me to the burger guy."

"Sure. Come on."

Devlin walked him around the back of the food kitchen, found Daggert inspecting some desserts. He looked up, a question?

"Fred, this is Jonas Kirk, back from the great northern arctic somewhere."

"Fred Daggert. Great display of treats," Kirk started, "And I can see why you're doing so well...I hear that you're even thinking of expanding your franchise in Woodland Park...that true?"

"Well, I guess if the word is out to someone who just returned from the Arctic, it must be true," Daggert smiled. "Yeah, we're looking for a new location...have some land in hand, but still not sure about traffic, accessibility, and the like. We'll just keep looking 'til we think we have the right place."

"Sounds like a plan," Kirk responded. "I just know that you seem to be doing everything right and people like your place."

"Well, thanks Jonas. Hey, drop by anytime and show the manager this card," he handed a small coupon to Kirk. "It'll let you eat a meal without charge...though be sure you don't let it slip into the hands of ol' Devlin here. I gave him one once, and we lost money that day," he smiled.

"I'll use it. Don't want to ruin your profit margin."

Daggert shared a laugh among the three of them. "Well, gotta get back to the main job. See you around, Jonas."

"For sure, Fred...for sure."

As they walked away, Devlin whispered to him. "Whaddya think about ol' Fred?"

"I think he makes good food."

"That's all?"

"Well, his coupon's seems good as gold."

"Whaddya mean?"

"See what he gave me?" Kirk held out his hand.

Devlin looked, "A coupon."

Kirk closed his hand moved it toward Devlin, then stopped and opened it again and asked, "What now?"

He opened his hand revealing a dollar coin. He grinned, "Will that get you a burger, Devlin? Eh?"

"Christ, Kirk. When you gonna get serious."

Kirk smiled, "Right now. Let's get back to our cards and win some money. I didn't like losing."

QUESTIONS

B 5

Examining a new reality. Sharing insights. Absorbing information.

Kirk walked into *Ole's Donut 'Ole* with a bit of spring in his step. Good night of sleep. Fun evening of Bingo. Met nice people. Had some ideas. Pretty good outlook.

He sat down, told Ole he was changing his morning order from apple fritter to iced donuts and coffee. Waited. Thoughts. Coffee arrived, pastry right behind. He sat and let his mind refocus. Sipped. Didn't want to burn himself... don't try to do too much with a single swallow. Not a bad approach to solving crimes, he thought. Took a bite of the donut and reviewed what he saw and heard last night.

Amused again with the saucy banter of Geraldine Wright. Every community needed a mouth like hers and she carried information that no one else did...she had Devlin...and she had the regular comings and goings that took her into various shops and several social meetings. Names kept surfacing in her conversation: Alice Goodwin, Victoria Blessing, Fred Daggert, Large Marge, owner of the fabric store. Geraldine knew a lot.

Seeing Sharon Cunningham engaged in a close, public conversation with Ahmed surprised him a bit. Since her return from India, she hadn't been associated with anyone. Then again, he had been away for a year. Things change.

Still wondered what happened with Father Lockhart in India. All those official explanations about him simply dying seemed a little vague. Maid showed up in the morning and he was dead. Reading candle burned to small nub...but no room fire, thank goodness. Someday, he would like to have a more candid conversation with Sharon, but right now, he wanted to learn a bit more about Ahmed, the Sikhs and their recent search for a temple. Could be a problem there.

Devlin's cache of secret information...evidence attached to the dead man's body...that was explosive. Probably not going to be able to keep that under control much longer. Gonna be a finding by a grand jury sometime, and "Death by person or persons unknown", would be a lot better than a report that proclaimed, "Victim of Muslim terrorism".

He let his mind rest on Tracy Metzger. His first impression...a low-life escapee from Iowa. Full of chatter, good at talking up a crowd, but hard to see him evolving into any kind of a significant player in the community. Here today, gone in about 6 months. Probably need to check into his background in Iowa. Heard that he had worked for two or three parishes down there in the past few years. Shifty, slippery...a loser. His Bingo number was probably L-00. He smiled at that.

Then, there was the Bishop. He could not help feeling that Burkey's arrogance and ambition were connected somehow to this community distress. Would he, or the Church perhaps, benefit if Devlin revealed that there was a Muslim connection to the death of the homeless man? Why did a Bishop attach himself so publicly to Bingo? Why was it that he popped up clad in formal vestments so often? Why no monsignor to assist him? Avoiding any oversight from an underling?

Well, no harm in taking a good close look at him. He had explored sensitive issues with Burkey before...found him a man of great ambition, arrogant and fully capable of slippery thoughts about both canon and criminal law.

Might be good to have a talk with Alice Goodwin. He heard her name mentioned two or three times in chatter last night. Close to the Bishop. Essential to the Altar Society. Liked to talk. A little hard of hearing, Geraldine had mentioned, but still, confused phrases could sometimes translate into a truth.

The bell on Ole's door rang out, a gust of much cooler air swirled into the tables, heads turned and there he was: Devlin. Scowl on his face, he glanced around, found Kirk's face, asked the counter for a quick order of four eggs, sausage, hash browns and side of pancakes. Came over and sat down.

"I'd like to say good morning, Devlin, but you don't look happy."

"I'm not."

"And why would that be?"

He lowered his voice a bit, "Another robbery last night... over at *Marge's Fabric Shop*. Break-in sometime between midnight and 6 am when there was no patrol on the streets...one of those Black Nights. Ol' Marge didn't lose much...she has taken to bringing home any large sums at the end of the day. But still, some cloth was taken, along with a couple of sewing machines on sale and some petty cash. It just pisses me off...big time."

"Do these robberies occur any night of the week?"

Devlin paused, thought a bit, and then had an answer. "Well, yeah, like I told you before, we get two-three attempts a week. Last time we caught one it was a petty crook who cracked into the pet store. We found him the next day trying to sell some birds he took away with him."

"So, the other robberies...a little more organized?"

"Well signs of it, yes...very skilled work in the successful ones."

"Do they happen on a Wednesday?"

"Hmm, yep, I think so. Would have to check the records to be sure."

"So what you're saying is that there are people out there trying to break in to business almost every night, but they likely only succeed on Wednesday. Wonder if those are the nights when there are no patrols out after midnight?"

"I can look."

"Well, Devlin, if that's the case, clearly there is some kind of leak in the police staff...the thieves know when there will be no patrol."

"We thought of that. We make assignments in a haphazard way, letting the staff believe that there will be patrols on every night and then about 8 in the evening, we let 'em know that no one has to work the graveyard that night."

"What's the interval between Black Nights?"

"Sometimes it's three-days, sometimes nine, sometimes six. We vary it. I'll look, but if someone is learning that a particular Wednesday is clear, they must be uncommonly lucky. And that doesn't account for all the other attempted break-ins."

"And you, on those Black Nights, you hang around the station all evening just to give the appearance of some kind of leadership presence, eh?"

"Yeah, usually for an hour or so. Then, if its Wednesday, I drop on over to Bingo to give everyone there the idea that the patrols are active. People see a cop at Bingo... they think there is probably police presence everywhere. Just seems like good public relations."

"Got it. Well, Devlin let me see what I can sort out."

"If you think of anything, let me know...I'm getting high blood pressure from this and I don't manage my blood sugar very well."

"While I have you here, let me shift the conversation to the murder at *Cold Stone Charity*. You interviewed Victoria Blessing, right?"

"Yeah...but I gotta say, Kirk, she is direct, unassuming, full of talk and happy to help us in any way she can. I'd testify all day long that she knows nothing about the murder other than that it occurred outside her building. She's still looking hard for a place to relocate her operations, but there isn't a harmful bone in her body...and she really doesn't have anything to add to what we know."

"So that night...the first night of the Bingo program... when the heavy snow started in early evening and socked things in for nearly ten days...that night, she saw no one, heard nothing, knows zero?"

"Well, she saw someone of course. Had a few shoppers between 5 and 6:30 pm...faces she knew, but no names. Then, Alice Goodwin dropped by along with the Bishop to bring some donations...visited with her for a while. Kept her a bit after closing time. Had some chuckles about the Bishop's fabric needs. As Victoria remembers it, Alice found his compulsion to wear his vestments and display his miter and crozier to be amusing. He was always looking for new things she could order through "The Roman Catalogue". He sure liked to dress up."

"Anything else from her about the Bishop?"

"Well, Alice did comment that he was not pleased to see so many Muslims moving into town...didn't like the Sikhs either...but in my opinion, that is just a little religious envy...though it may have triggered Wednesday night Bingo...just to invigorate the Catholic community. It certainly gives the Church a renewed sense of leadership in Woodland Park. For her part, Victoria finds him a bit vain, maybe amusing, certainly distracting I suppose."

"What time did she close up the night of the murder?"

"Near 7:00 when all was said and done. Alice and the Bishop kept her around till about a quarter to seven. She heard about the storm coming and wanted to get on over to Bingo. It was all quiet when they left...oh, yeah, the Bishop walked past the front door just looking at the foundation of the building, like he was shopping to buy the thing...came back in briefly to use the rest room. Wasn't in there long."

"And then, it got a lot more quiet, eh?"

"Damn right it did."

"Well, Devlin, it's not over yet. When you gonna release the evidence?"

"Not 'til I have to."

"Well, see how long it can keep. Give me a chance to do some work," Kirk smiled.

"I'll remember that," Devlin looked at his watch, "Gotta go. See what you can find out. I would like to put this homicide to bed."

Kirk watched the lieutenant shuffle through the tables and open the door. A fresh breeze swept in, even as Devlin stepped out. Kirk took a deep breath, sipped his coffee.

SEDUCTION

I 16

Revealing parts of the whole. A suggestion. An observation. A tease. Sharing a secret...connection...passion...purpose. Flavoring the ordinary with the unusual.

Kirk awoke the following Tuesday with a plan, a little complicated...but he thought he could see it through. Called Sharon Cunningham and set up an afternoon meeting at Ole's. Called Fred Daggert and made an appointment for 10 a.m.

He had an idea where these two conversations might go, but then, he told himself, until they happened, he could not be sure...could not take the next step. One thing...he didn't want Devlin in on any of them...might get sticky.

He pulled up in front of *ZigZag*, saw Daggert stepping out of the side entry. Kirk hit the horn lightly, waved him over and unlocked the passenger door. Fred eased in, smiling, thanked Kirk for the shelter and began asking questions.

"Well, Jonas, you said you had some ideas about local properties last night at Bingo," he began, "Was that something just for Sharon or maybe an idea that would work for me?"

"I'm thinking of something that might work for two or three parties here in Woodland Park, Fred. Let me just lay it out. I hear you are considering adding another franchise outlet in town. Victoria Blessing is interested in relocating *Stone Cold Charity* to a more accessible location. Ahmed Hassan and the Sikh community are seeking land upon which to build a temple. So, keeping in mind these interests, maybe a land swap could bring you all what you are looking for."

"Land swap?"

"Yep. According to city tax rolls, you have two parcels of undeveloped land here in Woodland Park. Offering to trade one parcel to *Charity*, you could expand *ZigZag* to their current location. That building is just about the right size for your burger operation. There's lots of traffic, easy access to streets, plenty of parking and it would place your franchise in a part of town that you can't serve right now."

"Trade values gotta be even, at least reasonable."

"Well, they would probably need a little cash sweetener, there's a building already there, you know, but I'll leave that to you and Victoria to work out. But my sense is that it balances out pretty nicely."

"Say they do," Daggert continued, "What does any of that do for the Sikh community, which I like incidentally. Ahmed is a quiet, confident leader...a born businessman to my thinking. But where do they come into this deal?"

"My thought is that you could make a charitable donation of your other parcel to the Sikhs. Inflate the paper value before you convey it, deduct it from taxes and give yourself a little more capital to remodel and expand the Charity site. Ahmed could take the donation, put it together with the funds they have saved, get a reasonable loan from the bank and build their temple."

Daggert sat silent. Kirk could feel him sorting through the idea, noticed a little smile, sensed him becoming comfortable with the entire package. Finally, he spoke.

"Well, I like it. The Temple donation is a plus for *ZigZag*. Builds community values and integrates diversity into our reputation. Might get a little cash flow from them too... could help underwrite a new location. Charity site has great traffic."

"Well, it's an idea, Fred. Now, I don't do business deals, although I saw my father put together a lot of them before he was killed. I think this one has real potential, and I'm gonna just let you pursue it. I think you'll find both Victoria and Hassan comfortable people to deal with. Fair enough?"

"I'm good," Daggert answered. He paused to think a couple of thoughts, then reached for the door handle. "It's nice to have you back in town, Jonas. You hungry? Want a couple of biscuit sausage and eggs?"

"Not today. Got a lot to do and I've had my breakfast. Let me hear how your discussions with everyone turn out. O.K.?"

"Yep," Daggert responded, smiled to Kirk, "Have a good day...you must be up to something important to pass up a free meal."

"Fred...you're right," and he laughed, started the car and waved goodbye. Headed for Ole's and a donut session with

Sharon Cunningham. He would cue her to what Daggert may be thinking and she could carry that message to the Sikhs. Then, he could speak his mind to her about the murder...well about the murderer.

On impulse, he stopped by *Marge's Fabric Shop* for a visit. Learned from her that the recent robbery at her place was more upsetting than it was a financial loss. Insurance covered her quite nicely, but the thieves left behind bad smells.

"Smells? What does that mean, Marge?"

"Oh, like someone walked through with greasy onions... just not pleasant."

"Burgers?"

"Could'a been."

"With or without fries?" Kirk smiled.

"Didn't find any...no spilled ketchup either...hell I don't know."

"Any recent sales to Alice Goodwin."

"She shops here from time to time," Marge commented, "Usually looking for something to decorate the Bishop's vestments and garb."

"Any recent purchases?"

"Oh, a couple. Sometimes she picks up some flattering fabric or maybe a bit of cloth with some real sparkle in it. He likes purple. She likes red. Tries to please him I guess, and as hard of hearing as she is, it probably smooths out a lot of their conversations."

"Thanks, Marge...say how're you and Geraldine getting along these days?

"Now, Jonas, don't leave me with a bad taste in my mouth. I nearly killed that damn woman when she started talking about my measurements being short...word get around about that and I'd have to shut my doors."

'Ever talk about it with her?"

"Sort of...I don't punch her out, and she stays away from my store. So, yeah, I guess we get along. I enjoy not seeing her...you know."

"I know. Well, check with you later, Marge. Keep your scissors sharp."

"Bad joke, Jonas," she smiled.

He left her in a good mood.

Next, Sharon Cunningham.

He arrived at Ole's just a little late, glanced inside and saw her in the back. Good. Private conversation.

He walked in, nodded to Ole and went to her table, smiled a hello and sat down. She acknowledged him with a raised eyebrow, let her mind run a thought or two as he settled.

"Jonas...welcome back to the sugar shack...want a fritter?"

"Sharon...really good to see you...no food, just some coffee."

"I'll wave 'em over...so, what's on your mind?"

"Couple of things I guess. "When you see Ahmed, mention to him that he should talk to Fred Daggert about a good deal on a piece of land. I think he may find the placement for his Temple."

"Jonas! Really!"

"He can just consider it a kind of personal investment in the community...Fred practicing good karma," he smiled.

"Well, Ahmed will recognize that. He's quite sensitive to kindness, part of what makes him so effective...and a bit magnetic, I think."

"He sure is. Seems to be well accepted everywhere," he muttered to himself.

"Anything else, Jonas?"

"Community stuff. Wanted to sort through some ideas."

"About what?"

"Well, murder I guess, although I have spent a little time trying to figure out those local robberies."

"They are a bit upsetting. Thieves seem busy two or three times a week, though most don't succeed. Then again, some do and those seem like carefully planned break-ins...almost as though they have inside information on when they can hit a local business."

"Exactly. Still, I find myself still focusing on that homeless guy dying there in the back alley. Really offends me...not an outsider random act. Gotta be local. Puzzling."

"Murder is always more compelling than robbery, don't you think?"

"Has been for me, Sharon. You know Woodland Park doesn't see much serious crime, so violent death...well, I get interested. Sort of an 'up close and personal' reaction, but it takes a while to sort out motive and means."

"Sometimes, there is no answer, Jonas. I've seen that. Death caused by fate."

"Well, sometimes a little distance can make a sudden death seem a bit more mysterious. Father Lockhart, for example. I never did get a good handle on what killed him. Fate? Was that it?"

Sharon Cunningham felt a jolt. Was Kirk sharing confidences or seeking convictions? She looked directly at him.

"He did die suddenly. You know, I had recently redecorated his bedroom before I left. He liked green décor, and I had fun doing it. Really surprising to me to hear of his passing."

"The Victorians used to do that a lot, then they discovered there was a lot of arsenic in that paste...had to give it up."

"Well, that's a century old bit of news, Jonas," Sharon replied, "My product was modern, no risk to it at all, but I will say that it was hard for me to be so close to him and have him die alone. Have you had any experiences like that?"

"Oh, I've had my moments. Not personal losses so much, but I've been near a few homicides that offended my sense of justice...when law enforcement failed. How about you, ever felt strongly enough to imagine permanently short-circuiting someone's life?"

"Well, so long as we are talking theoretical, yes...I've had my thoughts."

"Just curious, did they follow you to India?"

"Well, Jonas, there were certainly moments over there when I experienced some deep disappointments...on a personal level. How I reacted...well, sort of cloudy now. Not sure what my day to day produced."

"Yeah, India was a pretty long time ago now. How about the recent death of that homeless guy behind *Stone Cold Charity*?"

She grimaced, "Homicide is always so repugnant...hard to think about a man in the cold, looking for shelter and finding a deep sleep."

"Speculation? About who might have committed it?"

"I've had my thoughts, Jonas. We don't really know when he died...but I believe it was sometime that day before the storm hit...bet he was looking for shelter. Victoria Blessing says that there's a regular gathering of the homeless in bad weather...looking for wraps in castaway goods left in the alley. Can't buy the idea that the murderer was just a passing stranger...cold night, storm looming...no time to be wandering through the city."

"Anything else?"

"Well, Alice Goodwin told me that she and Burkey were shopping the Charity that night. She was especially amused that he was all dressed in formal garb because he was going to be "sanctifying" the first night of Bingo a little later in the evening. Even had a new sash that he kept adjusting to keep the tension just right. On the other hand, they arrived at *Cold Stone Charity* together and they left together...can't see Alice as an accomplice."

Kirk listened carefully, sipped some coffee, asked a question. "Still, if you were to hone in on Burkey as a suspect, Sharon, what would you be looking for?"

"Well...the weapon. All the talk about town suggests that it was a knife. No one anywhere heard any gunshots, though a few...Ahmed, Devlin, Geraldine...remember hearing a screech that night...figured it was a metal gate or maybe a rabbit in the talons of a night owl. But maybe it was a death scream? From where? Sound travels in all directions. Could have been behind the Charity? Hmmm. Maybe. But then, how does a Bishop dressed for the evening carry a knife...and where does he put it after the deed...if he did it?"

"Can I share something with you...confidentially."

"Go ahead...maybe I'll return the favor."

"Devlin confirms that it was a knife, long and sharp. But more, there was a note, in Arabic, stating 'God is Great'. That's the slogan of a Muslim terrorist. He also said that they found a small torn bit of fabric in the guy's hand."

"Well, that certainly isn't in the gossip pipeline...poor fellow."

"Quite sad...Say, anyone ever get the name of this victim?"

"I haven't heard one, Jonas. No one has come forward to report a missing person either."

"We should place dog tags on the homeless."

"Good thought. I'll send it on to the National Guard," she smiled...laughed. Then more seriously, "Hmmm. Torn bit of fabric, eh...wonder if it came from a Sikh turban...hmmm, probably not. They carry a short dagger in their headdress though...possible?"

"Yes, possible...but it was a long knife, according to Devlin...might have come from something a Bishop might be wearing, especially this one."

Long pause in the conversation, and Kirk used it to mull over just what he wanted to say next. Finally, he ventured a thought.

"You know...without evidence, even time of death really, we are left just speculating. But I am taken with the report that Bishop Burkey was certainly in the vicinity... looking over *Stone Cold Charity*, shopping a bit before he went over to bless the Bingo crowd."

Sharon Cunningham looked at Kirk with slowly narrowing eyes. She heard him, felt herself resonate with his thoughts. Wondered how far he was willing to go with this line of speculation.

"You know, Jonas, even if we could find convincing evidence tying Burkey to that murder, we would still have a problem getting any kind of a conviction. Would have to find the knife...would have to tie fabric to him...would have to find witnesses to nail down a time line for a murder that occurred when?"

Kirk noticed her use of the word, "we".

"I agree. There is a lot of missing evidence. And no real suspects. No one knows...for sure. Tricky. Still..."

She listened. She felt thoughts of India resurfacing... Burkey...the whole mess with Father Lockhart. What was Kirk suggesting?

"Just for conversation sake, Jonas, let's say that we tried to find evidence to link Burkey to the murder. Would the Church even permit a criminal charge and trial? Complications there. And if we got him before a court. Then what? How could one convict a Bishop of murder without a boatload of evidence? Right now, we have none...only speculation. If we began seeking justice, how would we even go about it?"

Kirk paused several seconds. Felt the barriers to candid conversation disintegrating. Decided to cross the line.

"I liked your method."

He left that remark sitting in the air. He had a suspicion about the death of Father Lockhart over in India. Sharon

Cunningham had been back in Woodland Park for months before he died. No apparent connection to the priest's death. Yet he had an idea of what might have happened. He continued, "I thought what you did was especially skillful."

She said nothing, felt a bit of panic rise in her, wondered what Kirk really knew about India. What could she share? What <u>would</u> she share?

"I don't have a repertoire for murder, Jonas, do you?"

"Well, I admired one homicide...bicycle rider died when someone loaded arsine gas into his water bottle...pretty slick...gas can be tricky to diagnose...and who knows how the victim was exposed to it."

"Well, that was you solving a murder. Far different matter to actually eliminate a killer from society."

"Oh, yes. But consider. If done well, it could be an unknown act. Death by circumstance."

Sharon Cunningham's body jerked. Her mind raced, panic twirling in her throat. A moment. She looked away, stalling an answer with what she hoped looked like calculation. Slowly, she brought her mind back into control of her thoughts. What did Kirk really want?

This was an exploratory conversation, had to be. Kirk was seeking candor, confidence...not an arrest and conviction. A partner of some sort. Was she to be one? Could she share India...any of it...all of it? Silence.

Finally, she spoke.

"Mmmmm...death by circumstance. Well, the circumstance came, I thought, from the hand of man creating a random act of God, eh. That was my thought, when I left India."

Ooooooh...there it was! Kirk felt a jarring thud in his gut. Held his breath a bit and then asked, at last, the question.

"And did they find out?"

"I'm still here, aren't I?"

Silence. They looked at one another, truth unwinding caution. He knew...and she knew he knew. Their eyes locked, neither wavered. Senses unwinding helter-skelter, they shared the quivering excitement of a secret so powerful and so tightly held that knowledge itself created instant intimacy.

Sharon Cunningham gave Kirk a hard, unwavering look... how would he see this revelation? She saw admiration, even appreciation in his face. She felt herself melt a little, shaking a bit as his approval swept over every pore of her skin. Unexpected, unsettling, sexually arousing, his reactions touched her deeply and with a slight shudder she saw Kirk expand his approval with a look, caress her courage, absorb her trust.

He reached across the table slowly, touched her hand, softly, "Yep, you're still here, Sharon."

More silence...as each of them wrapped their discovery package into memory, checked it twice to be sure it was safe. Slowly, she exhaled, let her mind drift into the mental embrace she felt pulsing from Kirk.

"Jonas...if I were a few years younger, I would probably help you search for a lot of things."

"Age is just a state of mind, Sharon. It adjusts to changing circumstances."

"A numbers game you think?"

"Odds and evens…a match."

Silence.

She felt the invitation. More, she felt her response.

"I'll keep that in my thoughts. Anything else to talk about, Jonas?" She smiled her warmest embrace, narrowed her eyes.

He smiled, rose from the table.

"What's your afternoon look like?"

"I'm going to have a conversation with Alice Goodwin."

"One less appointment for me, Sharon. I like working with you."

She smiled, "I like it too, Jonas." Her eyes narrowed a little more.

He felt the heat, "I'll be in touch…"

"I hope so."

He heard her.

ALICE GOODWIN

N 42

In every conversation there are words and there are messages. A good listener understands both. Careful now.

"Alice, this is Sharon. Been thinking. Some things I'd like to talk to you about...Altar Society stuff. Are you going to be available this early afternoon...we could smooze a bit?"

"Am I going to able *to take a snooze?* Is that what you need to know?"

"No, Alice. Well, maybe...I don't know. What I want to talk about should not interfere in a nap."

"Oh, I don't take naps."

"Are you alert now?"

"Oh, *sure I know how*...just relax and let the mind go blank for a few minutes...wonderful stuff."

"Let me try again, Alice."

"Oh, *I try to stay out of sin*...but what is it that you want to talk about, Sharon?"

"Maybe we should just meet, and I can explain."

"Oh, I'm sorry you're *in pain*...maybe we should just get together at Bishop Burkey's offices. He's travelling to St. Cloud today to meet with a collection of social workers. Such a good man...so invested in his flock."

"That would be quite fine, Alice, say 2:00 pm."

"Yes, I think *there is some wine.* Good time to see you."

Sharon Cunningham set her cellphone down gently, resisting the urge to slam it into the table. So maddening, trying to chat with Alice and having to guess what was going on in her mind. Well, she named a time and place amidst all of that, so that's good. And Burkey is gone for the day. Even better.

She rang the doorbell at the entry to the residence, and to her surprise, Alice answered.

"Ohhh, Alice...you got here early and alone?"

"Yes, today is the cleaning lady's day off...and I thought, what a nice setting...very quiet, I can hear better and we can have a good talk about whatever it was that you wanted."

Sharon laughed, "Well, our good fortune...couldn't be better. I am just a little curious about some of Bishop Burkey's habits, not the ones he wears, but his routine, his titles and such."

"Oh...my goodness, Sharon, *there is no secret to his vitals.* He's in very good health."

Sharon paused before continuing. "You know, Alice, sometimes I have a hard time putting my thoughts into longer sentences. I'm wondering if you would be willing to let me just ask you short questions and you could answer 'yes' or 'no'?"

"Oh, I understand that, Sharon. Anyway, sometimes I have trouble keeping track of phrases...my hearing cuts in and out. Let's try that."

Sharon paused, let that last sentence just linger. Then she began.

"Alice, can you take me to the Bishop's dressing room?"

"Why yes," and she turned and led the way.

"Is this where he dresses in his formal wear?"

"Yes. Start to finish."

"Can you show me his hanging clothes...robes, cassocks, gowns, and such?"

"Yes," and she led Sharon into a huge walk in closet.

"On the right, Alice, are those stacks of sash to be worn on different occasions?"

"Yes, although I don't know *all his persuasions.*"

"Mind if I look through them just a bit?"

"That would be fine. What are you looking for, Sharon, a special color or something?"

"Well yes...a fabric relatively new with a certain tone of red in it."

"Well, *some of them can carry a phone*, but most of them can't"

"Hmmm. Alice, has the Bishop purchased any new fabric recently, anything you might have used to sew a sash or two?

"*Fabric? Sash? New?* Oh, yes...but I send the bolts on to charity once I have made him one sash, never two."

"One sash and the bolt is gone?"

"Oh, yes. He is very particular about wearing distinctive official clothing."

"What about that sash you made him recently. Is it in here?"

"No."

"Oh, is he wearing it today?"

"No."

"Out for cleaning?"

"No."

"Can we take a look at it?"

"No."

"Why, Alice, why?"

"*He's not shy,* not really."

"Alice, what happened to the red sash you made him?"

"Oh, that sash. Well, I noticed when it came back from cleaning that it had a tear in it...couldn't keep anything like that around, so I just put it in the rag-bag and sent it on to charity."

"To *Stone Cold Charity*?"

"No, the charity of this month is the *Good Lord Clothing Center* in Minneapolis. They take anything, and they move things right out...gets into the hands of the needy almost overnight."

Sharon paused and let her thoughts take over for just a few moments. The sash was effectively gone. The fabric bolt was gone. Evidence was gone. Damn! Well, what about the knife...possibly still floating around here somewhere in the guise of a self-defense tool.

"Alice. You mentioned once that the Bishop carried a knife around with him in his crozier. How did he do that?"

"Oh, simple. It's a hollow staff. A solid one would be much too heavy to be carting around the way he has to go. The base is threaded, and he created a cap attached to a clamp. Put a very sharp knife in it. You know how he likes to lift and drop the crozier for emphasis when he is talking...takes quite a beating, but he solved that. He could just shove the knife into a pointed peg in the base, clamp it, and then screw the cap and that kept everything in place. He could pound that staff all day and the knife would stay in place."

"Hmmmm. I see it in the corner of his walk-in closet. Could you show me how that works?"

"Oh, sure." Alice walked behind the array of robes and gowns, reached in and brought out the staff. She turned it upside down, grasped the cap at the bottom and gave it a twist. It came off in her hand, but there was nothing attached. Sharon could see a clamp and a pin which might have been used to keep a weapon in place...but no knife.

"So this is where he places it, eh Alice?"

"Why, yes."

"It's not here."

"Oh, well then I guess he took it out for cleaning. He does that from time to time. Can probably find it in the kitchen."

"One more thing, Alice. I see the top end of the crozier, right at the beginning of the arc, has a dozen little perforated holes in it. Why is that?"

"Oh, if it were tightly sealed, the inside becomes really foul smelling. This way, incense, fresh air and such can enter and escape. He likes it smelling good."

"Really?"

"Oh, yes. He is a very fastidious creature of habit... well not a religious habit...not the nun's habit...oh dear, where are my words taking me...he is a very religious, decent man who is devoted to Christ and the Church... that is what I mean to say."

"Oh, Alice, I know exactly what you mean. Well, maybe the Altar Society could give him some special recognition... maybe get some more cloth for a special sash...resurface the coating on the crozier. How's his miter?"

"*He keeps a lighter* in his pocket, Sharon...doesn't smoke, but likes to assist those who might, and of course, he never knows when he will get a chance to burn some incense. He is so committed to his calling."

Sharon decided that she had done her best. Asked Alice if they could take a quick look for the knife in the kitchen. They went through the drawers and the dishwasher. Nothing.

"He may have sent it out for sharpening," Alice commented.

"Alice, you have been so helpful. Really gives me some good ideas on how the Altar Society could make a special gift to the Bishop. I may be back in a day or two, when you know he will be away again, and pick up the crozier. Give it a good polish. I'll bet he would love that, shiny new silver and gold."

She left Alice dusting some of the Bishop's furniture and went to her car. She sat there for nearly a half hour, sorting through information, reflecting on her conversation with Alice, feeling it disintegrate as she slowly picked up the sexual thread in her chat with Kirk. Not really sure if she should pursue that, but she was still unsettled, and it has been a long, long time.

What did she want from him, anyway? Excitement? The search for a murderer? To seal secrets with sex? Maybe just an interlude to satisfy curiosity and growing hunger... but not a commitment. A one-time thing. She was in the mood. He was there and open to it, she could tell.

142

Picked up her cell and called Kirk.

"Jonas...got a moment?"

"Oh, sure. What's up?"

"I think that I have found an answer to the homicide... and I may have a way to resolve it."

Kirk remained silent.

"You there?"

"I am."

"Met with Alice Goodwin."

"Worth it?"

"More than you can imagine. Where can I speak to you in private?"

He wondered if it were too soon...if she wanted to explore that edginess he felt earlier. Might as well find out.

"My place?"

She paused...thought about options, opportunities, strategies...her senses pulsed. Her eyes narrowed. "After supper...I have a dinner appointment with Geraldine."

"Good."

"Say 9ish."

"Perfect."

She paused, felt her face warming, her body stirring. She whispered, "Get a nap."

"Oooooo K."

He did. Stored energy. Renewed vitality.

She arrived. They said little 'til after midnight, and by then Kirk had a deeply centered, new appreciation for Sharon Cunningham. Some pillow talk, another diversion and then as dawn arrived, a new sensibility as they planned a strategy to bring justice to the nameless, cold, frozen corpse found behind *Stone Cold Charity*.

Bingo? Next week…eight days…Wednesday. Perfect.

THE SETTING

O 67

Slam the cue ball into the rack. Chaos! Chalk the stick. Sink the numbers. In order. Satisfying.

"Woodland Park Police Department, Detective Lieutenant Chester Devlin. Whose calling?"

"My God, Devlin, you sound like a polished professional... and yet I know you so well."

"Kirk...I am not gonna sit here and listen to you...just not gonna do it unless you have something I want to know... do you?"

"I think I may have an answer to your local robbery spree."

"Oh, really. You still sleeping...dreaming maybe?"

"I'm serious, Devlin, and I have a couple of questions."

"Go ahead."

"Is tonight one of those nights when the patrols will be off the streets after midnight?"

"Whose asking?"

"I am."

"Yes."

"Excellent!"

"Why, what do you care?"

"I think we can make a big hit on the robberies that have been surfacing around town...a little tricky to do it, but if you're willing to follow my strategy, we could do it, eh?"

"Explain, Kirk, and do it slowly. I'm not in the mood for fancy."

"Nor I." He laid it all out amid a series of Devlin grunts.

"Now, Devlin, can you do what I ask?"

"I can."

"All right. I'll get to the Bingo Hall about a half hour early and make sure that we can sit together. You get your team in place, and we'll enjoy the evening...maybe even win some money."

"I'll be there. We'll see about the other."

"We will indeed."

Devlin hung up the phone, took a moment to run through his mind the plan for the evening...smiled. If they came up with arrests, no one would care what the overtime cost. He'd be the talk of the town, and he didn't mind that at all. Well, for now, time to just execute. He hollered into the other room, "Oswald! I want to meet with the entire squad at 6 pm...sharp. Not a word about it to anyone else...just bring them all in."

"Will do, Lieutenant."

Devlin liked the sound of that response. Liked being called "Lieutenant".

Kirk smiled as he closed his phone. He enjoyed Devlin's feistiness, took genuine pleasure in seeing him publicly recognized for his arrests. He himself certainly didn't need it...didn't want it. Quite enough to be in the cast and let Devlin play the lead.

Then, there was the other thing...the Bishop. Sharon had invited Burkey to come by at intermission, bless the Bingo crowd and thank everyone for the good things that it had produced. He agreed. Excellent.

It all seemed safe...justice for Burkey wouldn't bring credit to Devlin...but that was fine. He smiled. Tonight's Bingo would be remembered in Woodland Park for years to come, but who wanted to be responsible for that.

He thought about Sharon Cunningham. Not easy to find someone who shared his view on justice...but she certainly acted on her convictions in India. Nothing he felt he had to balance on the scales of justice. Outside his jurisdiction. Not a member of his tribe. Simply a punishment for betrayal. He admired that. Smiled. He still felt her hands on him, lethal in more than one way.

Then his mind focused...she said that he needed to meet her before 2:00 pm and things could get underway. Timing close, but it could be done...would be done.

While Kirk got himself together, Sharon Cunningham acted.

"Hello, this is Alice Goodwin. Who is calling?"

"Hi Alice. This is Sharon, got a minute?"

"Well, *don't want to be in it*, whatever it is."

"No, no, Alice. Can I meet you at the Bishop's quarters? You mentioned earlier that he would be in meetings all afternoon. I'd like to bring by some cleansers that I think would polish up his crozier and make it shine a bit more. He said he would address the Bingo crowd tonight...thanking everyone for the growth and income of the games."

"Yes. He'll be there...he mentioned that to me, talked to Tracy too. Said he would show up at the intermission. And sure, you can come by now. I'll meet you there."

"Thank you, Alice. I really like working with you."

"My pleasure, Sharon. *I like joking with you too*. See you soon."

"Right away, Alice."

She touched off the phone, checked her watch and drew a breath. If Kirk had completed his task, they could get this in place. She drove out to his home, walked in without a knock. Intimate.

"Jonas...you there?"

"I am."

"Did you get it?"

"I did."

"Where *are* you?"

"Just arriving," and he walked out of the hallway that led to the garage, and handed it to her, "I think it's gonna work just fine."

She glanced at him without expression. He winked and smiled. She ignored it. That took him aback. After last week, he expected to bask a bit in an afterglow. Nothing there.

"Well done," she said smartly, "I'm on my way to meet Alice now. I'll let you know soon as I'm finished."

"Work carefully," he glanced at her to see if they were sharing an intimate purpose. Didn't see anything.

"Oh, I will. I know about this stuff," she said in a businesslike tone.

"See you at Bingo?" He looked again to see if there was a message in her eyes, her body. He saw nothing.

"Oh, yes. I'm not going to miss this."

Without another word, or look, she turned, leaving Kirk as though he were now kindling in her woodpile. Harvested and set aside.

Maybe that was it. A night. A time. A departure. No commitment, no promises. Well, that worked for him. Memories were nice to keep...far better that they be singular than that they be troublesome.

He lay down to take a nap. He was gonna have to be alert tonight…for Bingo of all things. He smiled and drifted off to sleep.

THE REVEAL

B 53

A little thought. A subtle placement. Formality withers in the face of the unpredictable. Solutions surface. Conundrums remain.

Chatter and clatter. Incessant. Happy reports about Bingo had circulated for weeks throughout Woodland Park. The crowd grew. Card prices increased. *ZigZag* sales at the hall doubled and daily income increased 10 percent at the restaurants. Fred Daggert had to add new employees. Weekly growth in revenues allowed Father Eggert to negotiate a new contract with *Stone Cold Charity* allowing it to provide expanded care for the homeless, and the *Gazette* announced on the front page that *ZigZag* was trading properties with *Charity* giving both better locations to pursue their business.

Ahmed Hassan sat quietly in the hall, arriving early in the hope of spending a little time chatting with Sharon. While he waited, he mulled over the business offer that Fred Daggert had offered him. It would essentially put his people into a parcel of land Daggert owned in return for a modest ten-year stream of revenue from the Sikhs.

The financial commitment, reasonably limited, could be met without restricting construction and maintenance of their Temple. What not to like? Good karma. He scanned the crowd hoping to see Sharon. Not yet. He kept looking.

Kirk arrived early, saved a chair for Devlin, got himself a cup of coffee, settled in with four cards and waited for Tracy Metzger. Sharon arrived about 6:50, glanced at him, nodded slightly and went directly over to visit with Ahmed. She didn't appear to be leaving his side anytime soon.

Devlin arrived to a series of greetings from old friends and some antagonists. He absorbed it all and sidled over to his seat next to Kirk. They exchanged looks and Devlin just nodded. Kirk relaxed a little.

Father Eggert stepped out behind the curtain promptly at seven pm. He welcomed everyone to the fun, accounted for the success of St. Mark's Bingo and turned the evening over to Tracy Metzger. In spite of himself, Kirk found his body tightening up again. He was confident that one criminal would be behind bars tonight. He was not so sure that the other one would be dealt with in any meaningful way.

Metzger greeted everyone with a big smile, a loud "hallo" and an Iowa joke. "I was at the Miss Iowa Beauty Contest last year," he commented. "No one finished first, but there was a tie for third place."

The laughter turned to a roar. "That Tracy," Devlin grimaced, "He really does know how to keep a crowd happy. Wonder if he'll be laughing by morning.

"Relax, Devlin. The best is yet to come."

And the games began. In an hour, as the crowd was getting a bit restless, Metzger announced one of the two special games for the evening, and then "we'll break for food and drink".

"It's the 'Ten or Out' game, folks. You know how it works. I draw ten numbers. If there is a winner, the prize is gonna be $500 tonight. Special jackpot. O.K., everybody ready."

Silence.

He began calling the numbers:

N 34; G 47

Metzger kept making the calls, the last three putting everyone on edge. Room became very silent.

I 17...anyone got a Bingo? Anyone? No. O.K. next number...

O 63...silence.

O.K. last chance on this special jackpot...here's the number:

B-53..."Ouch! Gotta get glasses," Metzger commented, "Number is G-53."

Groans, then a burst of talk...frustrating anguish once again.

Kirk jumped when he heard that number, B-53. That was it.

He turned to Devlin. "Anyone ever won one of these "Ten or Out" games?"

"Not when I've been here."

"Not surprising, I think."

"Why. Is it fixed?"

"No, not by men, but the odds of a win with just 10 numbers drawn are astronomical...it's just a little tease of a game."

"No chance?"

"Next to none. I ran it by a statistician at the university... never gonna be a winner...not in our lifetime."

"Well, I'm not looking for luck, Kirk. Want an answer to these robberies. If you're wrong, I'm gonna be the laughing stock of the department."

"I think you're safe, Devlin. I've heard all I need to hear from Metzger.

Now, here comes the Bishop. Soon as he has done his thing, we can all go get some food. Listen up...maybe he'll say something important."

"Well, that would be a first by His Honor."

"You address him as 'Your Excellency' Devlin."

"I don't."

Kirk smiled, turned to watch the stage.

Bishop Burkey stepped out from behind the curtain, his purple and white gown rich and full in the interior light, a bright red sash wrapped 8 inches wide further emphasizing his authority. He raised and lowered the crozier, dropping it smartly to the floor. A distinctive thud.

His height seemed unusually striking with the miter set atop his head. Marked in red and purple, it seemed to teeter with nary a totter. He nodded to the altar boy walking alongside, gently swinging incense, letting the smoke curl into the close air, presenting the aroma of holiness and sanctity.

He paused, and in a dramatic gesture, slowly raised and dropped his crozier on the hard surface of the stage again. It thumped loudly, resonating throughout the hall. Voices stilled; heads bowed. He dropped it a third time, seemingly captivated by his ability to quiet a crowd to hear the word of God, or at least the word of one of God's servants.

He looked around the hall, slowly, turning his head an entire 180 degrees to ensure that he had the attention of all. He was after all...a Bishop. Then, satisfied, he stepped forward three more steps, held the crozier close as though he could cling to God's power by keeping the symbol of the shepherd next to his body.

He raised his right hand to bless all who had come to celebrate God's purpose, holding his posture in case anyone wanted to snap a picture. As he began to move his arms in the sign of the cross, his eyes began to roll. He paused. Shook his head very slightly, then refocused, keeping his right hand elevated. As he began that traditional greeting, its motion seemed to set him at sea, rocking. His arm paused. His body began to sway. He took a half-step to steady himself. Then another.

A worried moan came up from the crowd. The crozier left his hand and clattered to the floor of the stage. Still committed to his task, Burkey regathered himself, again raised his right hand to convey God's blessing, and this time, it failed to rise about his shoulder. He tilted again, then collapsed into his robes as though he were emptied of air.

Devlin turned and looked at me.

"What the hell is going on up there?"

Kirk had no answer for him.

Devlin worked his way to the stage, pushed on-lookers aside and took a look at the Bishop. Felt for a pulse... scratchy, erratic. Touched his skin...cool and cooling. Called for the electro-cardio unit that St. Mark's kept available at all public gatherings. Shocked the Bishop once...then again. Pulse stronger, color still faint, sepia almost.

He looked at Kirk, "Call 9-1-1. Now!"

While Devlin worked, Sharon Cunningham carefully gathered the miter and staff, waited for the EMT ambulance to leave, then collected Alice Goodwin and drove directly to the Bishop's quarters.

"I'll make sure that the crozier is cleaned up, Alice. You put all his clothes in order the way he likes them. He may make it...we can only hope."

"Yes," Alice responded in tears, "He may."

He did not. It was well after midnight when the Bishop, still struggling to regain consciousness, finally relaxed one last time.

By then, Devlin and Kirk were nestled in an unmarked patrol car, waiting radio alerts. They came, finally, at 2:30 am, reporting a group of three found working through the windows of the *Quick Snacks Gas N Go*. Quickly arrested by the cops working overtime, they blamed it all on Tracy Metzger.

Devlin demanded to know just how that could be, but they said nothing more and Devlin sent them off to jail, still puzzled.

"Well, Kirk, one way or another these guys were getting info on when the streets would be empty of cops. Got any ideas?"

"I do."

"Care to share."

"I do."

"Is this the time?"

"It is."

Kirk paused, arranged his thoughts and began.

"Here is the scam, Devlin. Metzger is directing a small group of thieves who intentionally make false break-ins during the week. Odd days, no schedule. Point is to lead police to believe that a crime wave is trying to gain traction. But that's risky. An actual break in might lead to arrests. So, amidst the false efforts, they focus on the night when the graveyard shift will be cancelled. Then, they get right to it, for real."

Devlin just looked at him, mind cranking out possible objections. "Well, maybe I could buy a few broken windows and forced doors as planned failures, but how does Metzger know when there are no cops on duty...that it's o.k. to send them out for real burglaries?"

"He knows it's a Black Night when you show up for Bingo. You told me that you only go when there's no overnight patrol. My guess is that there is a lot of casual conversation about your occasional appearances, Devlin. I could imagine Father Eggert mentioning it to Burkey, or even to Metzger. Maybe Geraldine dropped the strategy in a gossip session somewhere. Whatever. Once you were in the audience, Tracy knew it was a safe night and he could signal his group, all of whom were there serving food for *ZigZag*."

"What signal? What's he gonna do?"

"He calls out a Bingo ball that doesn't exist."

"What the hell does that mean, Kirk, 'a Bingo ball that doesn't exist'. If it doesn't exist how can he call the number."

"It's a slippery trick, Devlin. Most people don't really think about it, but every letter has a range of numbers associated with it. "B" for example has numbers 1-15. No others. The sequence for "G" is 46-60."

"You know this how?"

"Trust me, Devlin. It's the structure. The sequence for "N" is 31-45. Run a test."

He looked at Kirk hard, squinted. "Well, I'll buy it, for now. So, what's the signal?"

"He calls the nonexistent number: B-53."

"And then?" Devlin asked."

"Then his merry band knows that the streets are clear that night. I've been taking note of those "Big Jackpot" calls at two different sessions and twice I heard B-53. Once they hear that number called, even if Metzger corrects himself, the gang hits the streets. Tonight, you were waiting for them."

Devlin looked at him, shook his head. "You...how...? Never mind." He took a few moments to repeat to himself what Kirk told him. Needed to be clear when he talked to the press. Better make some notes.

Kirk smiled. Well, this would play well with the *Gazette*, but the paper was gonna be more interested in what happened to the Bishop.

It was. Next day's afternoon headline: *Death Comes to the Bishop: Hospital Says Heart Attack.* It went on to review Burkey's career, his commitment to foreign missions, his energy in creating new sources of income, his talent for presenting the faith in the flowery finery of his robes and miter, crozier too. Terrible loss.

A front-page sidebar revealed more: *Devlin Beats Bingo Code.* The Lieutenant's face warmed as he read how he and his team broke up the local robbery team that Metzger had organized and directed. The Crime Wave was over. The article went on to say that Father Eggert planned to restructure the staff and St. Mark's Bingo would resume within the month. Fred Daggett stated that he would replace lost Bingo staff with Sikhs, creating more employment diversity.

Below the fold, the *Gazette* carried a final police report on the death of the homeless man found under the snow weeks ago. *Cold Trail Frozen in Place,* it reported. While lamenting the lack of suspects in the death of a stranger, the Coroner was left with an unexciting verdict. "Homicide through stabbing by person or persons unknown."

The publisher ordered a record run of the day's issue. In Ole's, there were constant high fives and great praise for Devlin. Some began to call him "Chief", a name he warmed to. The gossips chattered not at all about the cause of the Bishop's death.

Sharon Cunningham made sure of that. Long before the paper hit the streets, she and Alice had begun sorting the Burkey's clothing and tidying up his working desk. Sharon took the crozier into the courtyard, carefully removed the lethal container, put it into a plastic bag, and later dropped it into the garbage bin outside *Westside Liquors.* Alice arranged the miter and plumped its edges. Together, they searched for the knife usually kept in the base of his staff. It was missing...a puzzlement, so they checked the kitchen dishwasher to see if he had run it through the latest wash cycle. Nothing.

"Well, it was like him to put things away from time to time. We'll probably find it as we clean out the rectory," Alice commented.

"He could never rest in peace if things were in disarray," Sharon agreed.

"Oh, my no he would not," Alice, near tears, chimed right back, "He would *be so dismayed.*"

Sharon shook her head, smiling. My secret is safe with Alice, she thought.

It was quite a secret. Representing himself as an adjunct to the local police, Kirk had examined a pressurized cartridge of arsine gas from the microchip factory where it was used in production. The cartridge had a very soft, thin rubber diaphragm at one end. A little conversation...a slight-of-hand substitution of the Radio Shack cartridge he carried with him...and he was out of there...delivering the poisonous cylinder to Sharon.

She used the clamp in the bottom of the crozier to set the capsule so that it gently touched the base peg. Every time Burkey pounded his crozier into the floor, the pin punctured the rubber diaphragm, allowing compressed arsine gas to fill the hollow staff, overflowing through the holes near the crook, silently filling the Bishop's breath. Lethal.

Sharon smiled. Death by circumstance. Nothing to confess there.

She wiped her memory clean and began imagining a fresh week with Ahmed reassuring him that the temple was a sound project, pressing against him as they examined the plans, serving him evening meals that fit his diet and enhanced her presence. "Life is good...and getting better," she thought.

On the third night of their first week together, Ahmed looked at her carefully, appeared reluctant to speak. Were there worries? "What is it, Ahmed? What disturbs you?"

"I am surprised with my feelings for you, Sharon...and with myself. My faith says that I should lie with no woman if she not be my wife. Yet here I am. I am not certain how to account for this. Is this fair to you?"

"Oh, Ahmed, there's a truth to life that is often beyond rational sense, beyond faith." She moved her hand across his chest, "Be thankful for whatever it is that binds us so closely. Who knows where it may lead us? If it will endure? How it may end? Accept what life gives us, and if it's not forever, let it at least end honorably...that is very important," she said as her eyes narrowed, "It must end honorably."

"Sharon, I do not find its end in my thoughts...nor will I."

"As you say, Ahmed."

"And what of this man, Jonas Kirk? Is he a friend to you, or a rival to me? What is he to us?"

She draped her arm over his shoulder, letting her hand work through the lengths of his hair, roaming as she whispered. "Oh, he just wanders, Ahmed. He gets in and out of trouble in a way that only the rich can manage. He can disappear overnight and not be back for months. We'll see him when we see him. He has nothing to do with us."

Ahmed tried to give Kirk another thought, without success. Sharon Cunningham's hands distracted him. Her body soon absorbed him. He said nothing more.

Midnight now, and she let her mind just settle. Another night with her man. A quiet week. Safe. Secure. A community at peace. An opportunity for the Sikhs to settle in. She sighed with satisfaction. She and Kirk.

Quite a team, she fancied herself a bit as Lady Justice. He embraced the identity of Mr. Scales. He did the one thing she couldn't...acquire arsine gas. She did what he couldn't, load the crozier.

The Bishop did the rest. A public venue. A chance to do his song and dance and then...she smiled...

BINGO!

Printed in the United States
By Bookmasters